AS THE GEARS TURN

TALES OF STEAMWORLD

PATRICK THOMAS

PADWOLF
PUBLISHING

For Erin and Colin

PADWOLF PUBLISHING INC.
WWW.PADWOLF.COM
www.facebook.com/Padwolf

WWW.PATTHOMAS.NET
www.facebook.com/PatrickThomasAuthor

AS THE GEARS TURN
Tales of Steamworld
© 2016 Patrick Thomas

-Deadly Imitation was originally published in Clockwork Chaos edited by Neal Levin and Danielle Ackley-McPhail
-The Banks of the City Thames was originally published in Tales of the Talisman magazine
-That Voodoo That You Do was originally published in In An Iron Cage: The Magic of Steampunk, edited by Danielle Ackley-McPhail, Elektra Hammond, and Neal Levin

Book edited by John L. French

Cover Art by Patrick Thomas and Roy Maurtisen

Cover Design by Roy Maurtisen

Jackson Grimstone, The Spellpunk. Lady Thistle, Sir Bult, The Knights of the Steamtable, Lil Repute, Colonel Windglass and the Skyrovers. Steamworld, Playworld and all related characters are © & TM Patrick Thomas

This is a work of fiction. No similarity between any of the names, characters, persons, situations and/or institutions and those of any preexisting person or institution is intended and any similarity which may exist is purely coincidental.

10-digit ISBN 1-890096-65-2, 13 digit ISBN 978-1-890096-65-6
Printed in the USA
Second Printing

CONTENTS

Jackson Grimstone, the Spellpunk

in

DEADLY IMITATION

The livery driver knew he had a customer by the crick of the door and the slight sinking of the back of his buggy as someone sat down.

"Evening Guv'nor, where to?" asked the driver, craning his head behind him. As soon as he saw the bald man in the stovetop hat, he cringed.

"Oh no, not you. Get out of my cab, Grimstone."

"Careful there, Stevie, your cockney accent is slipping," said the passenger, a mischievous grin on his face.

"Look, I have to put on a show to fit in here, but I don't have to do it for you. Get lost. Every time I see you, it's nothing but trouble. I wish I was back on Earth," Stevie said.

"I don't," Grimstone said.

"Well, yeah that's because you fit in here. Back home before we were taken, I was pulling down six, almost seven, figures a year as a broker. I was on my way to a lingerie model trophy wife. Instead of living the best years of my life drinking body shots and banging a beautiful woman every night before retiring at thirty-five to a tropical paradise, I end up here. Worse, I'm stuck with you and the rest of these backwards cretins, none of whom even realize that they're part of a stupid playworld. Back home I could have bought and sold you. What were you, a chemistry teacher in a high school?"

"Physics," corrected Grimstone.

The cabby kept talking as if Grimstone hadn't answered. "And here you're notorious and rich. And what do I do? I have to drive a livery cab to survive. I hate horses. And with the Thames city subway, I never get long runs, just short rides— there's no money in the short rides. Hell, I can't even afford one of the autos here and they're not even real cars. The damn things run on steam same as the trains. And those giant gears in everything are ridiculous. They don't even try to miniaturize anything."

"It's part of the world's Steampunk motif. That's how things work here. And you are hardly an innocent. Weren't you wanted for bilking some sweet old ladies out of their savings?"

"Indicted. Never convicted."

In the shadows of a nearby alley, something stirred. A man dressed in black pulled a pistol out of his inside breast pocket and pointed it at Grimstone. Before the muzzle could line up with the bald man's head, Grimstone had already slipped a knife out of his sleeve and flipped his wrist, catching the would-be assassin in the throat with the throwing blade. The assassin was caught by surprise. His last sounds were a gurgle of blood as he fell back into the wall and slid down to the pavement, his gun falling harmlessly to the walkway.

"Holy shite!" yelled Stevie. "What the hell did you go and do that for?"

Grimstone didn't answer. Instead he linked his hands behind his head leaned back and put his feet up on the front seat of the cab which was built to hold four passengers, two in the front and two in the back.

"Get the hell out of my cab! You just killed that guy. I'm not going down for murder."

"Not murder. Self-defense. You'd think Baron Rogan would get tired of sending men to kill me and have them die senselessly in the process."

"How'd you even know he was there?"

Again Grimstone stayed silent but adjusted the goggles he wore. He'd managed to come across a pair of goggles in another playworld that had motion detectors, night vision, telescopic, and microscopic abilities, along with a host of other visual enhancements.

"You can sit here and argue with me, but eventually someone will notice the corpse and call the cops. Do you really want to be here when they start asking questions? We both know you're a buck and do more than drive this cab to make ends meet. You've crowed a few jobs and you run goods for the dollyshops.”

"Hey, a guy's got to make a living," said Stevie, shrugging.

"Exactly. Which is what I'm trying to do. So if you would so kindly take me to Tenth and Dorchester, we can both get on with what we do."

The driver grumbled and mumbled under his breath, but snapped the reigns so his horse started pulling. They rode most of the way in silence until they passed a small boy on a corner hocking papers.

"Read all about it! The Spellpunk stops opium smuggling ring!" shouted the boy.

"Stop," ordered Grimstone. The cabby grumbled, but pulled back on the reigns and the cab and buggy came to a halt.

"Boy, I'll take one."

The boy ran over to him and held up the paper in one hand, his other palm outstretched for a coin. As he looked up at Grimstone, his pupils went wide and he glanced first at the cover of the paper and then back at Grimstone.

"You're him. You're the Spellpunk."

"Actually he is me, but it's not really worth arguing the point."

The boy, more than a little awed, broke with his normal practice of making sure he had payment first and handed the paper over.

Grimstone reached out his hand to drop a coin in the boy's palm. The boy, a tiny bit of fear on his face, said, "No charge, Sir. For you it's free."

Grimstone put his hand to his pocket and put the coin away and took out another.

"Nonsense, my boy. You have to make a living, just like the rest of us. And this job helps keep you out of the orphanages and the factories, I assume."

"Actually, it's me and my mums, sir. We rent a room over on Locke Street."

Grimstone put a coin in the boy's hand. When he saw it a huge smile came across his face. "Sir, that's a gold pony— twenty-five sovereigns. I wouldn't make that much selling papers in a year."

"Put it in your pocket and keep it hidden. Consider it a tip and see if you can't get some better housing for you and your mother."

"Yes, Sir. Thank you, Sir." The boy took off his hat and started bowing. "If you ever need anything, Sir, me name's Falkner. I'm at your service."

"Thank you, Falkner. I will keep that in mind." Grimstone snapped his fingers once. Stevie grimaced but started up the horse.

"I've driven you around close to a hundred times and you've never given me anything near that as a tip."

"When I think you've earned it, I'll give it to you. Now be quiet. I want to read about my latest adventure."

"But you were there. Don't you know what happened?"

"Sure I do, but the papers tend to make up the details they don't know. I always find it interesting to see how it compares to the real thing."

As the cab neared its destination the driver pulled up short. "We're here."

"I said Tenth and Dorchester. That's a block away."

"The coppers are all over down there. You get off here, Grimstone."

"Really?" said Grimstone, holding his hands up to his mouth like he was about to shout. "Squire, I think you should check under the driver's seat. There a hidden compartment with…"

"Shush! Fine, but not a word to them, okay?"

Grimstone didn't reply and the cab moved slowly down the street until a kid of about sixteen dressed in a police squire's uniform held up his hand to stop them.

"Sorry, but this area is closed off for a police investigation. You'll have to turn back and go around."

"Oh well then. Nothing to do about it, we'll get out of your way," said Stevie, all too happy to listen.

"Actually, Squire, I'm expected. I'm Jackson Grimstone."

"The Spellpunk. No one would lie about being you, but

I was not informed that you would be arriving. I will let you through, but you should know that Sir Roderick is in charge of the investigation. Should you not be expected, things will not go well for you."

"Duly noted, Squire. Now step aside and let us pass."

The crime scene was in an alley near the cross streets. The cab took him as far as the police vehicles.

"Good riddance, Grimstone," said Stevie.

"Such a harsh way to speak to such an old friend." Stevie snorted and made ready to leave. "Don't be going anywhere just yet. I will need a ride when I leave here."

"Find yourself another cab. I'm off duty."

"You will wait for me."

"And exactly how do you plan on making me do that?"

The men's eyes met. Stevie tried to look dark and menacing. Grimstone simply smiled, but it was not a happy grin and, in reality, the slight upturn of his lips was far more menacing than Stevie could manage to be with his entire body. The cabby broke eye contact first.

"Fine. I'll wait."

Grimstone opened the door and stepped from the cab carrying his cane with him. It wasn't something he needed to walk. It was partially for show, carved from rare black ivory that was tougher than steel. It took a skilled craftsman weeks to make just the dragon's head handle using diamond tipped tools. It was a weapon disguised as a walking stick. Instead of using it in the normal fashion, Grimstone held the bottom and put the upper end on his shoulder as he strolled jauntily toward the dead and bloody body of a young woman. His arrival did not go unnoticed.

"Grimstone, you get away from the body," Sir Roderick said. The knight was a big man both in height and girth, not so much fat as large. His strength was legendary, often being called in to single-handedly break up fights among a dozen or more men. His dislike of anyone who wasn't a fellow Steam Table Knight or a cop was as almost as well known. On his list of those he disliked, Jackson Grimstone probably held the top spot. "What the blazes are you doing here?"

"Sir Roderick! A pleasure as always. How are the wife and children? Haven't eaten the wee little ones yet, have you?"

"Grimstone, that is enough of yer mouth. Leave before I bodily throw you back into the gutter where you belong."

"Well, that is certainly something you and those big arms of yours might actually manage if I decided to let you. However, then you would have to explain why you did that after I was asked to come here and lend you my assistance."

"Who would ask you to come here?"

"Why, Her Majesty of course," Grimstone said.

"You're bluffing," Roderick said, as a small metallic sphere hovered around him. The gawker had a large lens making it look like a metallic eye was floating to one side of the knight, turning back and forth between the two men as they exchanged barbs. "As you can see I have the matter well in hand."

The knight had a sense of pride that the gawker had been following him. The flying spheres had a tendency to be around when interesting things happened. Of course, Grimstone was the only one nearby who both knew and was troubled by the curse of "May you live in interesting times."

"Showboating for the Bugeyes and their little cameras? Roddy, it's so beneath you."

The big knight began to look nervous. "I'm not ... what are you talking about ..."

"Oh come now. We both know your alien masters watch life through the gawkers."

"Grimstone, be silent!"

"Yes, yes. I know the Steam Table Knights are aware of the existence of the Bugeyes and know this world is merely a stage for them to watch. One of many, in fact. They have forgotten how to live so they choose to live vicariously through others. That's the truth, even if you are under orders not to let the populous know. But there are rumors. They see the gawkers and the robotic tourists. They suspect the truth. The Bugeyes may be able to set hoops on fire and force us to jump through them, but you don't have to look so happy about it.

Personally, I try to put a sausage on a stick when I have to jump in order to at least get a hot snack out of it. However, if you don't believe me about Her Majesty, why don't you send one of your squires to a call box? Or contact one of your zeppelin watch stations and find out if I'm speaking the truth. If I'm not, you're welcome to try to send me back into the gutter, but even if you do I shall be looking toward the stars."

The knight looked at him confused.

"A bastardization of a quote from Oscar Wilde."

"Who?"

"A writer you shall sadly never have the pleasure of reading."

The knight was not happy, but he called up one of his squires and sent him to a call box. The lad returned soon after, informing Sir Roderick that Her Majesty, Queen Theodora, had indeed requested Grimstone's assistance.

Grumbling the knight motioned for the Spellpunk to follow him. Roderick nodded to a squire who lifted up a sheet, revealing a butchered and bloody young woman, her crimson soaked clothes a scandalous outfit of a lady of the evening.

"This is the fourth girl we've found this month. They have all been ladybirds, each of them cut up in similar fashion with a blade."

"Damn Bugeyes. So obsessed with The Ripper that they can't get enough. And so they make more. They choose to prey upon the weak-minded."

"Are you saying the *aloff* are behind this?" whispered Sir Roderick.

"They are behind everything, pulling puppet strings, putting schemes into place that might not play out for years just to entertain their sick, twisted masses. Or haven't you noticed that every few years there is a new knife-wielding killer that has to be stopped?"

"I admit I do find it disturbing."

"The Bugeyes take a child, make sure he is abused and then arrange for a patron to adopt him so he may rise up in society. More often than not, the boy becomes a doctor. Although I admit this is the first one in some time that has focused on the ladies of the street. Do you have any witnesses?"

"None yet, but the squires are still canvassing. Not one clue left behind as to who or what did this."

"So Sir Roderick, what are your plans to catch this murdering bastard?"

"We will put undercover knights in the areas where the judys frequent. We were thinking of taking most of the women off the streets and closely watching the few that we allow to stay on in order to set a trap," said the knight.

"Sir Roderick, on a personal level I may find you to be a bore, but you are a quite a decent cop. I will help you set the trap, but it would hardly be chivalrous to put a young lady at risk. Perhaps we should provide other bait."

"Not a bad suggestion," said Sir Roderick.

"I'm glad you agree. Which one of us do you think should dress as a woman? Personally I would love it to be you, but you may have to shave that lovely handlebar moustache and we may have to convert a tent into a dress."

The knight scowled at Grimstone. "I was thinking more along the lines of using one of the squires. Many of them have not even grown their first beard and could more easily pass as a woman."

"It makes sense, but hardly as much fun as getting you in a dress. Where shall we dangle our bait?"

"All of the murders have been within a mile of this spot, although none have repeated locations. That leaves only two areas for the unfortunates to be."

"Then we best get working to get our plans in action. Shall I ride to the zeppelin watch station with you?" asked Grimstone.

The knight grumbled, almost growling. "Fine. Shall I send out of the squires to dismiss your cab?"

"Nah," Grimstone grinned. "I'll go tell him."

The Spellpunk walked out to where he left Stevie, but the horse and cab was nowhere to be found. He turned to the squire keeping people out of the area.

"Did you send off my cab?"

"No, sir. He took off like a bat out of Hades the moment you were out of sight."

"Bad Stevie. Going to have to find you later and teach you a lesson." The Spellpunk rejoined Roderick.

As night fell across the city of Thames a different element took to the streets, especially in the poorer neighborhoods. Some were criminal, most were not, at least in the strictest sense in that they were not actively engaged in illegal enterprises. These denizens of the night were concerned with the pursuit of pleasures, whether they be of the flesh, mind, soul or a mixture of any or all of the three.

True to his word, Sir Roderick had set up traps in the most likely areas to catch the latest Ripper. Both he and Grimstone decided to wait at the most likely spot. Hours passed without so much as a customer browsing, let alone partaking of the secret and carnal pleasured being laid out for sale on the shadowy street corner.

"This isn't working," Grimstone said, tapping his shaved head with the dragon's head. The gawker floated down as he spoke. "And I told you to back off out of sight or I'll melt you down for scrap." He pointed the tip of his black cane at the gawker and it floated behind some ivy on the nearby building.

"And why isn't it working then, being you have such great expertise on the going and comings of prostitutes and their clients," Sir Roderick said snidely.

"Other than your mother, I'm not really acquainted with many in that line of work," Grimstone said with a wag of his eyebrows. The knight offered a growl to the Spellpunk's grin.

"You still haven't told me what wrong with my trap," said the knight.

"What's wrong? Besides you dressing them all in pink and giving them parasols?" Grimstone asked.

Sir Roderick shrugged. "The parasols seemed the best way to hide the fact that they weren't really damsels. And the pink was to make them look more girlish."

"In the entire time we've been here, not one paying

customer has come along and met with any of our 'girls'. It probably looks too suspicious."

"And how do you propose we fix that, Grimstone?" Sir Roderick asked.

Grimstone tilted his hat jauntily to the side, covered up the dragon top of his cane with the palm of his hand and strutted merrily toward the squires in women's clothing.

The Spellpunk staggered slightly as if he had a bit too much to drink but not so much as to be incapacitated. The gawker floated out to follow, but Sir Roderick grabbed it with one meaty hand.

"Regulations or not, if you blow this trap, I will crush you myself," the knight whispered. The gawker floated back behind the ivy, but its lens adjusted to keep Grimstone in a close up.

The Spellpunk made his way across the street and put a hand on the wall in front of which one of the squires in girls' clothing was standing as if to hit on "her". And hit on her he did.

"Good evening, sweet lady. What will a crown and a loaf of bread get me?" The lad seemed horrified. It was the same squire that had let Grimstone in the area that the police had quartered off earlier in the day.

"Grimstone, what are you doing? This is very unseemly," the squire whispered, as his eyes darted toward the hiding places of his fellow coppers, embarrassment not only storming his face but taking up a stronghold there that it appeared ready to defend against all comers.

"Nonsense. The lot of you aren't fooling anybody. You're supposed to be out here to make money, yet you're horrified that I am trying to engage your services. You put aside those Victorian mores and act like a judy. You should be working hard in an attempt to disengage me from my money, which means you don't pull away. You lean forward, you smile, you laugh. You put a giggle in your talk and a wiggle in your walk. So what we are going to do is you are going to take my arm and we are going to walk around the corner as if I were a real customer and we were actually going to do what's needed in order for there to be an exchange of currency. That would make the lot of you look more likely to be prostitutes and less likely to be coppers."

Grimstone lead the squire around the corner, stopping once to squeeze his bottom. The squire almost clobbered him but managed to stay in character. Sir Roderick had seen the logic of the Spellpunk's plan and had sent a cop to engage the services of another of his undercover squires. They too walked off, but around the corner on the other side of the block. A single squire was left alone acting nervous, which was good for his cover. A woman alone on the streets at night would be anxious. It wasn't long before a man in a long wool coat and a hat lumbered down the street towards the squire. While it was not exactly a sweltering summer evening, it was not nearly cool enough to justify the scarf the man wore around his neck and face. Or the cloud of fog that seemed to follow in his wake.

"How much for the rest of the evening?" asked the man in the scarf, his voice sounding like it was coming from down a well.

"A crown," said the squire in a falsetto that cracked only slightly. His gentleman caller didn't seem to notice.

The scarfed figure reached in the pocket and handed over the requested amount. "Now come with me."

"Where are we going?" asked the squire.

"I'm not paying you to ask questions. I told you to come with me, whore," barked the scarfed figure. The squire seemed at a loss. He didn't know if this was the killer, but he didn't necessarily want to go off with a man who wasn't, especially since he had no intention of providing the services that were paid for. His hesitation lasted longer than the scarfed figure was willing to wait, so he reached out and grabbed the squire by the wrist and pulled. The squire tried to pull back, but was unable to break the grip, so he took a swing at the side of the man's hat with his parasol, which had the added value of being a large wooden club with metal inside to give it added heft. Sir Roderick hadn't wanted any of his squires unarmed. The blow should have at least stunned the man. Instead, all the squire got for his trouble was an ominous sounding metallic clunk.

The scarfed figure strolled away, dragging the disinclined squire in his wake. The lad at first stumbled and then ran in order to keep up. Sir Roderick held back until he saw the scarfed man reach into a special pocket on the side of his long woolen coat and pull out a long metal blade. He blew once then three times rapidly on a whistle and the Steam Table Knights moved in. Eight men, two knights and six squires, rushed the man. Each was equipped with their own specially weighted club. Dozens of blows rained down faster than hail during a spring storm, none of which affected the scarfed figure in the slightest. Next, the men tried to wrestle him to the ground and were tossed aside like rag dolls for their trouble. The only thing the melee accomplished was knocking the killer's hat off and tearing his long coat, revealing a silver metallic body beneath.

"Blazes, it's a tourist!" Sir Roderick snapped, moving in himself. Although the knight was a giant among men in both strength and bravery, he was a weakling when compared to the might of a metal man. The knight did his best to pin the mechanical arms to the tourist's side but his grip was broken and he too was tossed aside.

The gawker had left its ivy perch and followed, moving in for a close-up of the mechanization. The tourist swiped at it, but the sphere dodged it easier that a horsefly avoiding an old mare's tail.

Both Grimstone and the undercover squire had returned to the scene running and breathless.

"What do we do?" asked the squire. Instead of answering, Grimstone reached his hand inside the neckline of the squire and down into his brassiere. "Grimstone, what the hell are you doing?"

Grimstone put his hand out and with it the four pairs of socks that the squire had used to augment his chest size. "Figured you wouldn't need these. How far away is the nearest zeppelin airship?"

"Five minutes or so," said the squire.

"Go contact them and get them here."

"On whose authority?"

"Mine. Remember, the Queen asked me to poke my nose in. Tell them to pilot right over me and drop anchor, minus the anchor. Trust me, in the long run, Sir Roderick will thank you. Now run," said Grimstone, tossing one pair of socks aside before sneaking up behind the tourist and the three exhaust ports that were hooked up to his back. Grimstone shoved a pair of socks in each. He raised his cane over his head and used the tip to push the stockings further in. The tourist continued to move, although much more slowly.

"What did you do?" demanded the mechanical automation.

"You Bugeyes can project your consciousness into these robots, but you're foolish enough to bind yourself to the themes of this world, meaning you are allowing them to run on steam-based technology. That means I block your exhaust pipe and you have to slow down."

"You can't stop me. No human can match the strength of a tourist," said the automation. Stepping forward, the machine seeming to actually be straining with the effort and pushed harder until its internal pressure built up and two of the three pairs of socks were shot out of the exhaust tubes like woven cannonballs.

Grimstone stuck his cane between the tourist's legs as the mechanization took his next step. The result was a very ungraceful fall that brought the unfortunate squire the tourist was holding down alongside the mechanization. There was a trough meant for watering horses on the front of a nearby building and Grimstone ran towards it. Sir Roderick had a similar idea and followed him. The two men picked up the trough, carrying it between them back toward the tourist, although even Grimstone would admit that Sir Roderick bore most of the weight. The automation was back on his knees when they dumped the water down his pipes.

The water ran all over the automation but the robot was waterproof except for his exhaust pipes, which quickly filled up, the water pouring down into the section that burnt coal specially designed to last a day without needing to be replaced.

The water should have been enough to put out the fire within and stop the automation from moving.

Unfortunately, the steam-powered Ripper didn't seem to be playing by the rules because even as the fire within burnt out his limbs began to become active again.

"What the blazes is happening?" Sir Roderick said, bending forward to try and pull the automation's leg out from under him to knock him back down. The tourist only wobbled.

"Obviously, he has managed to modify the mechanical shell," said Grimstone. "A clear violation of the rules that govern visitation of the playworlds."

"How do you even know that? Not even the Knights are privy to that."

"This isn't the first playworld that I've visited. Or the first privy, which is where the Bugeyes belong. But this is the one they've hidden my daughter on, so I'm staying until I find her."

Grimstone looked right into the gawker's eye lens as he spoke. "And then I'm coming for the ones that did this to us." He turned toward the tourist. "Now if you don't come quietly, I'm going have to report you. Oops, I think I have. They don't take too kindly to rogue tourists, do they? Throws off the whole entertainment dynamics. Can't have the camera fodder catching on and getting ideas of their own, can we?"

"And just how do you think you can do that? No one from a playworld can visit our home," said the tourist.

"True, but I can always phone it in. Or I guess telegraph it to be more era specific. Or did you miss the floating broadcast center up there?" Grimstone said, pointing to the hovering gawker.

Instead of showing worry, the consciousness hosting robot laughed and waved at the floating globe. "Hello out there!" The mechanization turned back to Grimstone. "Yeah, I may be in all sorts of trouble, but if I'm entertaining and get good ratings all will be forgiven. And what could be better ratings magic than killing the notorious Jackson Grimstone?"

"Jackson Grimstone kicking your mechanical posterior I'd imagine, at least if the number of gawkers stalking me at any given time is any indication."

Grimstone rammed his cane into the wrist joint of the hand holding the squire and the grip loosened. The Spellpunk pulled the boy in a dress free. "Go on and get yourself out of here, Miss. This is man's business."

Grimstone laughed and pointed his cane at the metal hand with a knife. A single electrical blast shot out, temporarily shorting out the hand so when Grimstone hit it with his cane, the knife fell to the cobbles. "Back home that comment would have gotten me in trouble with the PC police. And several women far more capable than I'll ever be."

The tourist rose to his feet. "I've watched you. You criticize me for cheating, but you have knowledge of higher level tech, making people think you have magical powers and using it to your advantage all the time," the tourist said.

"And there is no time like the present," said Grimstone, pulling a handful of large marbles from his pocket and tossing them on the ground where chemicals mixed with each other and the air, creating large clouds of smoke. "Now you see me, now you don't."

The mechanization swung his arms wildly in the haze. "Just because I can't see you doesn't mean I can't kill you."

"But it does help my odds a wee bit, don't it?" the Spellpunk said, his voice suddenly above the tourist.

"What?" the tourist yelled, craning his neck upwards in time to see Grimstone soar by. "You can fly?"

"Under the right circumstances," Grimstone said, wrapping a rope tied lasso-style around the chest and under the arms of the metal visitor. The Spellpunk yanked twice on it. "Going up."

With a lurch, the rope tightened and the tourist launched upward, his legs clearing the ground in an instant.

"What the hell?" the tourist said.

"I control the powers of light and darkness. Simple levitation is well within my powers," Grimstone said.

"You of full of shite. You control nothing," the mechanization said, craning his neck back to see the outline of a zeppelin soaring above them. "You think lifting me off the ground will stop me? I'll climb up this rope and rip your head off and piss down your throat."

"See, this sort of thing is why we don't allow tourists to use our plumbing facilities. You're just too dumb to figure out how to use a water closet."

The tourist reached up and pulled on the rope with one hand, then the next.

Grimstone wagged his finger at the mechanization. "I wouldn't do that if I were you."

"You're not me. I'm smarter," said the tourist.

"That remains to be seen," said Grimstone, taking a swipe with his cane at the floating gawker who had followed them into the sky before putting his walking stick in his mouth. Both hands free, he ascended higher up the rope with the mechanization following behind.

The tourist climbed slowly and steadily behind the scrambling Grimstone, quickly closing the gap. Grimstone reached the side of the airship and shouted, "Permission to come aboard."

"Granted," boomed a deep voice and the Spellpunk scurried over the hull.

"Grimstone, in a moment I will be onboard that airship. Then I'll kill you and scuttle it," said the tourist.

"Not really on the agenda for today, old boy." Grimstone pressed the dragon's left eye and a long blade sprung out of the cane's end. Grimstone slipped the blade under the rope.

The tourist was not close enough to grab hold of the hull, so he looked down, amazed at how high the airship had climbed in so brief a time. "No!"

"Oh yes," said Grimstone, slicing through the rope.

The mechanization plummeted down more than a hundred meters, crashing in the walled section of Ireland Yard. Tourists were built tough, but not indestructible. The impact snapped one of his legs, making it difficult to stand, which made it easy for the waiting knights to pull out a prod from a generator as big as a large cart and shock the tourist's system into shutdown mode long enough for them to shackle it.

"Smart move, heading toward the Yard, Captain," Grimstone said.

"Daring move, catching him in the noose like that," the airship captain replied. "Can I drop you back by Sir Roderick, so the two of you can head to the Yard together to finish the paperwork and the tourist's incarceration?"

"That would be wonderful," said Grimstone, looking down and seeing a familiar horse pulling a familiar cab. "Actually, I have a better idea. Do you have a spare anchor line?"

Moments later, Grimstone was again dangling below the airship, this time his foot in a loop, so he only needed to hold on to the rope with a single hand. The airship lowered so Grimstone was gliding above the busy street in a straight line for the cab.

"Oh, Stevie!"

The displaced cab driver looked around to see who could be calling him, then looked up and behind to see Grimstone descending toward him like a flying spider.

"No! Get away from me, Grimstone!"

"I told you to wait for me, Stevie, and you didn't listen. You best stop now while I'm in a forgiving mood," yelled Grimstone, his smile so wide that bugs were getting caught in his teeth.

Instead, Stevie cursed and urged his horse to greater speeds as if the devil himself was chasing him.

The next morning papers featured not only the tale of how the Spellpunk stopped a murdering tourist but how he flew through the air to catch a cab driver who had done him wrong.

Lady Thistle

in

THE BANKS OF THE CITY THAMES

"Tell me what you saw," asked the elfin knight cop wearing body armor and matching long coat.

"Well, Sir Thistle…"

"It's Lady Thistle."

"But you are a knight of the Steam Table and knights are all to be addressed as 'Sir'."

Thistle smiled. "As the first female knight, the Table is having to learn to make adjustments."

"That's an understatement," whispered the human Sir Bult, her reluctant partner and mentor.

The elf smiled at her frowning superior officer.

"Can't you just use magic to catch them?"

That caused Bult to have to muffle his laughter.

"Neither magic nor science works that way. Please tell me what you saw during the robbery."

"There was a man and a giz. The man wore all leather, a long coat, goggles, and a mask. He had a stovetop hat and a cane. The giz was about three meters high and twelve meters long with a mouth as big as a large child," the bank manager said.

Lady Thistle's pointed ears wiggled. "Are you trying to tell me that your bank was robbed by a mechanical dragon?"

"That's exactly what I'm telling you."

"Would I be safe in assuming you would recognize the dragon giz if you saw it again?" Sir Bult asked.

The manager nodded. "I'll never forget that gizard's metal teeth if I live to a century. Or the way the steam shot out his nostrils and or how his joints creaked. But I wouldn't recognize the man if I bumped into him on the street. There wasn't a bit of skin showing."

The knights interviewed the rest of the employees and the customers that were in the bank at the time of the robbery. Their stories matched up. The man only carried his cane, which he pointed as if it was a gun, but didn't use it. Why bother when he had a dragon at his beck and call?

"Do you think it could really be a giz dragon?" Thistle asked when she and her partner were alone.

The older knight shrugged. "It's possible. A few were rumored to survive the Zigat War. Sightings are rare. Any giz that size would have to stick to wild, open spaces. Too many gear hunters are looking for a trophy on the wall or to reverse engineer the things. Useless since they are more magic than tech."

Bult raised an eyebrow daring his protégé to contradict him. Thistle held her tongue. The senior knight was Thistle's mentor, although most of the time the knight felt like Thistle thought she knew it all. Bult worried that that kind of attitude could get her hurt, killed, or worse. None of which would help his career any, all things considered. Still, she was one of the brightest rookies that he had ever been paired with and her knowledge of gear tech was beyond most of the Steam Table's senior master gearers.

"I'll have to check with the airships and Steam Table HQ…" A modern miracle of a building that combined gear and spells to hover above the city. "…to see if any of them spotted a gizard flying away. It will undoubtedly be in the reports if they had. Okay, rookie, what else could be mistaken for a giz dragon?"

"Not much organic. Have to be gear. Maybe one of the Lord Engineers survived Zigat and built something new."

Bult smiled. "You're forgetting magic."

"Oh pish. There is no such thing as magic."

The older knight smiled. The Steam Table often teamed a gear knight with a spell knight. Each believed their way was the best, but most knights at least conceded the existence of the other specialty. Thistle refused to acknowledge that magic was anything more than science that she simply didn't understand yet.

"If it was truly science, there should be some way of taking apart amulets and figuring out how they work."

"That's because you are thinking in terms of the science we have today. It's all gears and steam and caged lightning. I'm thinking that there are ways to make things smaller. Perhaps so small that they cannot be seen by the naked eye. We both know there is science greater than that of the Table."

Bult shushed her and quickly turned his head side to side to make sure no one was close enough to hear.

"You know very well that is secret. No one outside the Table can know about it."

"The Table and the Royal Family," Thistle corrected.

The Steam Table kept order in the city of Thames and the country of Grand Albion. The Table answered to the Queen. The nobles and the common folk assumed Queen Theodora answered to herself and maybe to God if he was having a good day. The fact that there were those to whom even the Queen answered was a closely guarded secret, even if it was widely suspected because of the gawkers and tourists.

A small sphere floated in the door of the bank to take up position between the two knights. Sir Bult put his head in his hand. "Oh criminy. I have not had so many of these damn floating nuisances following me around since I was forced to take you as a partner."

Thistle smiled and shrugged. "Just lucky I guess. They have been trailing me around on and off since I was a child." She turned to the sphere and waved. "Hello. I was beginning to get worried. I hadn't seen one of you in weeks. I had started to think my life had gotten too dull for you to bother wanting to watch."

Bult slapped her elbow. It was commonly believed, but not confirmed to the general populous, that the gawkers were the eyes of something beyond this world and they followed people around to chronicle their adventures for the amusement of others. The Steam Table Knights knew this to be true but were not permitted to enlighten anyone else about it.

Thistle turned back to him and smiled one of those infuriating smiles. Infuriating because even on him they were very disarming and also because she usually was on the right end of things.

"Any chance of you tracking him?" Thistle asked.

Bult held up his tracking amulet one last time. A golden glow shone out to check the area. "No. The crook didn't leave behind any hair or skin for me to use."

"What about the giz?" Thistle smile had become smug, bordering on insubordinate.

"Spells don't work on gear, as you well know."

"Because there are no genetics for the amulet to trace. Sounds a lot like science to me."

"We have work to do," Sir Bult said gruffly.

Lady Thistle nodded and exited the bank in her own unique matter. Sir Bult sighed heavily. The senior knight had spoken to her about it again and again but she pointed out that nowhere in the regulations was there a rule that prohibited a knight from skipping. He planned to have it added in at the next conclave.

Each week brought more bank robberies. The dragon had begun using an internal flame thrower to keep the people in line. The cane of the Dragon Master, as the press were calling him, turned out to have some magic of its own. The Dragon Master would point it at the vaults and it would work through the wagon-wheel sized combination locks to open them so he could get more valuables.

It had turned from a curiosity into a manure fest. Banks were not insured so the money and valuables that were stolen could not be easily replaced. There was no requirement that the bank do so with the valuables stored in the vault. Money was another matter. Two banks had applied for insolvency because of their losses. The zeppelins that were set up across the city skies had indeed spotted the giz dragon on numerous occasions. The dragon flew out of the city, usually in one of three different directions. The dirigibles gave chase but even at their top speed, they were far too slow to catch a giz designed as a machine of war. And even the special reinforcing of the airships against arms fire might not be enough against the dragon's breath. The Table was getting pressure from both the nobles and the business community to put a stop to it. The losses were astronomical, hitting all levels of higher society. Many of the banks had taken to hiring their own security forces, including so-called freelance knights, each of whom wanted to make his name by slaying a giz dragon. So far three of them were in Queen's Hospital and two of them were in the grave, although those two were pushed directly into the gizard's flame by the Dragon Master. Oddly, many of the witnesses seemed to feel the dragon had shown restraint and halted the fire once he realized the two men were in its path. There was another case where the man ordered the giz to fry a portion of the crowd, including a woman holding an infant. The dragon refused and was soundly battered in the head by the man, a totally ineffective move but the machine made no move to strike back. The knights found this curious as a gear of that size should not be afraid of a human or anything else.

"We may be dealing with a mighty wizard here," Bult said.

"Or a mighty scientist," Lady Thistle countered. "If we can figure out what hold the man has over the giz dragon, we might be able to free it."

"Free it? We need to have a way to destroy it," Bult said.

"Say we were able to engage it in an attempt to demolish it, with a giz that size what is a likely estimate of damage, both in property and lives?"

"If we don't stop him more lives will be lost. Of course, neither way matters if we can't find the monster."

Thistle and Bult were not the only knights on the case, but the gawker continued to follow them. Many methods had been tried, including sending teams out into the wilderness to track it down, while others set traps within the city. All had come up empty.

"We need to figure out which bank will be hit next. There aren't that many branch offices left in Thames that haven't been robbed. There are only four offices that have escaped the robbers' attention. Of these, two are branches of a smaller bank that has not been robbed yet. Each of the remaining pair are owned by a bank that has been robbed. I suggest we pick one of the latter."

"Why?" Bult said, in full mentor mode.

"It seems odd to me that all banks but one have been hit."

Bult nodded approvingly at the younger knight. "The same thought had occurred to me. And that while this giz has been spotted leaving the city, no one seems to have seen him entering. I find that more than a little troubling. An invisibility spell of that magnitude would use much energy."

"I think it's using more mundane means. Either somehow it is somehow folding itself up in order to fit on a wagon or carriage or it is coming in through the sewer system."

"Good thinking, Thistle. Although it might be coming in through the subway tunnels as well. We will have the squires set up checkpoints at the city gates and the railroad stations. Which branch would you set a trap at?"

"Dawes Fiduciary Bank is rumored to have more in its holdings than the other. If I was going to rob one of the two, I'd pick that one."

"A knight rob a bank? You should not even say something like that jokingly. You must do nothing to tarnish the reputation of the Steam Table, even in jest."

"Yes, Sir Bult." He could not tell if the stoic look on the elf's face was because of actual regret or the strain of holding back a smile.

The manager at the Thames Gold and Loan was more than happy to allow the knights on the premises, hoping that their presence might deter the robbers. Neither knight bothered to tell them that they did not feel that their presence would deter anything. The gawker floating in the knights' wake should have been enough of a clue for the manager to figure that out.

Two days of waiting finally paid off. The robbers were not known to be subtle. The knights knew something was up when the front doors and several feet of the surrounding walls around them exploded inward. The goggle-wearing Dragon Master strode in, tipping his hat to the ladies as if he were at a ball.

"Ladies and gentlemen, there is no need to panic so long as you do what I say."

The man held several large sacks, most of which would be too heavy for a single man to carry once filled with too many valuables. The robber had oddly stayed away from all paper currency as if he knew that the serial numbers could be traced. This further raised the knights' suspicion against the owner of the un-robbed bank as it was something that few outside of banking, finance, and the Table would actually realize.

"We are just going to take a few valuables and most of the vault and then we will be on our way. As long as there are no heroics, no one will get hurt."

"I'm afraid I am going to ask you to lay down on the floor and put your hands behind your head," Sir Bult said, stepping forward.

"It's about time some of you Steam Table boys caught up to me. With your reputation, I thought it would happen much sooner than this. I guess those stories of skill, bravery, and inner fire about you coppers are just a lot of hot air. Speaking of hot air and fire, you should stand down or prepare to be incinerated."

"I don't know about that."

Lady Thistle moved in front of the dragon, holding a large container. She poured a vial of liquid into the larger canister, shook quickly, and tossed it down the dragon's gullet. The gawker floated in as close as it could without risking being bitten. Foam erupted going down the giz's metal throat and out his mouth.

"Little something I've been working on. A chemical extinguisher for fires. The gizard won't be making any flames for at least a half-hour until he can manage to fire his pilot light back up."

The giz began to move in such a way that it looked like he was trying to cough and vomit the white foam. More extinguisher just took take its place.

"Maybe longer," Thistle said. "And you forgot the Table girl in your calculations."

"Oh, you mean the Table's elf lass mascot. Not even a consideration in my plan, little girl."

Bult stepped forward, his fist connecting with the man in leather's jaw, knocking him back. "Your mistake. Underestimate that woman at your own peril. Trust me on that."

The man in leather rubbed his jaw. "Good shot, but not good enough."

"Don't worry, I have more." Sir Bult lifted a dagger from its sheath and pointed it at the robber. Lightning surged from the tip into the man in leather, causing him to stagger back.

"B-e-tter, but still not enough." The robber pointed to his boots. "Rubber soles." He pointed his staff at Bult and the knight flew across the bank as if the steel on his uniform was being thrown by unseen hands. "I think it's best I take my leave of you." The robber ran toward the dragon. "Get us out of here!"

The dragon withdrew his head from the hole his tail had made. The man in leather hopped upon the dragon's neck and with the flapping of his mighty metal wings took off into the sky. The knights ran into the alley, leaping onto their steam cycles, which was the Table's replacement for their steeds of old. At least in the city. In the country, some knights rode giz horses.

"We have to catch them before they make it out of the city." From a pouch on his bike, Sir Bult took out something that looked like an unusually long flintlock pistol and aimed it above the dragon. A gunpowder rocket soared past the escaping robbers and exploded in a burst of light in front of them.

"That should call in some backup," Sir Bult said.

"I have a plan. You follow them. I'm going to try to circle around in front of them," said Thistle, slipping a large pack onto her back. Sir Bult nodded and the two knights sped off in different directions. The gawker stuck with the lady knight.

Predicting the flight path of a dragon was not the easiest

thing to do. Thistle did figure that it would want to avoid the dirigibles as they were armed and able to fly. That meant they would be going right over Oak Hills. Thistle opened up the throttle on her steam bike, going straight up Tower Lane. It was the steepest street in all of Thames. Only the most experienced carriage driver could make it up easily. That meant it was usually empty and today was no exception. She could hear the approach of Bult's bike and hoped she could time this correctly.

Once on the top of Tower Lane, Thistle could see the dragon was only twenty feet above her. She leaped off the bike while pushing a control switch she was holding in her hand. The twin canisters on her back roared to life propelling her up into the sky on an intercept course. The metal sphere kept up with her ascent without any noticeable effort.

The man in leather was so intent on getting out of the city and avoiding the knights chasing him that he didn't notice Thistle until she was almost on top of him. The impact knocked the so-called Dragon Master from his seat. Thistle grabbed hold of the dragon's neck, letting go of the switch. The sky pack cut out. With her other hand, she grabbed for the man in leather, knocking the hat from his head. The only thing she managed to grasp hold of was his mask which slid off, leaving robber and knight cop face to face. The man in leather nodded with a grin and he peeled off his coat, holding the sleeves and the bottoms together. He dove off the dragon and the center tore open as a small parachute mushroomed out. It slowed his descent, enabling him to land on a nearby rooftop. His landing was hard but not so much that it stopped him from getting up to run away. The gawker followed him down to get shots of his escape.

Back in the sky, the dragon turned his head to look at the knight in an attempt to figure out why she was not attacking him. The gawker returned to watch the airborne drama unfold. Thistle lifted one hand off her grip and waved at the giz.

"Hello," Thistle said in greeting. The dragon nodded his head. "So how is this going to work?"

"I suppose you try and kill me while I attempt to throw you

to your death or perhaps rend you limb from limb," the dragon said.

"Doesn't really work for me."

"That makes you unusual for a knight."

"I guess I am. I'm the first woman to ever achieve the rank of Knight of the Steam Table."

"You're a female? I really can't tell just by looking at you. I tend to go more by the clothing. As you were wearing slacks and not a skirt, I assumed you were male."

"I'm not sure if I should be insulted or not. I have a theory that your partner in crime there was somehow was forcing you to help him. Am I correct?"

"Perhaps, but why should I reveal anything to you?" The giz turned to glare at the gawker. "Or anyone else."

"Because Knights of the Steam Table have a reputation for honesty and helping those in need."

"Not when the one in need is a giz dragon."

"Good point. Perhaps we can change that today. After all, you were dying, weren't you?" Thistle said.

The mechanical beast twisted his head and his eyelids squeaked as they narrowed. "How would you know that?"

"It is the only reason the *aloff* are put in a giz instead of a tourist. As I understand it, even among your people, life in a mechanization is preferable to no life at all," Thistle said.

"So you are knowledgeable. That does not infer honor. The Steam Table has fought to destroy all of the greater giz both during and since the Zigat War. Why should I trust a knight?" the dragon asked.

"Maybe you have no reason to, but perhaps you have a reason to trust me. Do you know Fyewal?"

There was more squeaking as the giz's eyes narrowed further. "I am familiar with her."

"I am a friend of hers. Have been since I was a little girl."

The dragon smiled, showing rows of steel teeth. "So you are her little one. Fyewal claims you once saved her life." Thistle nodded. The giz looked down at the mechanical body it was trapped in. "Such as it is."

"Let me do the same for you. I think I've figured out the hold he has on you. That's not armor strapped around your neck, is it? It's an infernal device, isn't it?"

"Yes."

"I can try to get it off of you."

"But that might make it explode. And if it does that you no longer have to worry about defeating me."

"True, but if the bomb goes off while I'm working on it, it will kill me too."

"An excellent point. Do you think you can get it off?"

Thistle wrapped her legs around the dragon's neck and hung upside down twisting so she could see the bomb attached to the lower length of his throat, ignoring the height that separated them from the ground far below. "The lock looks simple enough. I think I can do it."

"Then free me from this madman's control."

"Certainly, but in exchange, I would like your word that you will stop robbing banks and will take no retaliation against the city for this one man's actions."

"You would take a giz at his word?"

Thistle nodded.

"Very well you have the word of Samat."

A voice boomed out of the metal canister strapped to the dragon's chest. "Kill the knight. She saw my face. And bring her back so I can see her body."

"Radio transmission. Very impressive," Thistle whispered. "We're currently working on handheld versions so the knights could call for help no matter where in the city they were. We have them in the call boxes now. The transmitters take up about a cubic meter worth of space. Judging by the size of this, I assume he can't hear you?"

"No, but he claims to be able to detonate the bomb from wherever he is. Do not worry, I will not kill you. Those two men were not my doing."

"I know."

The radio boomed again. "You have one minute to be in the

skies over where you know I am. If not I will end you, gizard."

"You'd best go. I have no desire to take anyone else with me. And I cannot kill someone who tried to help me. I'm tired of all this. Death will be a release." The giz looked at the gawker. "Perhaps it will even entertain those back home."

There was a click and Thistle pulled the metal collar off the dragon. "No need. I got it." By this point, they were outside of the city so she dropped the collar into the London River. It exploded as it struck the water.

"Now how about we take care of the bank robber," Thistle said.

"Revenge?" the dragon asked.

"Justice," the knight answered.

Abercrombie Pennsburg was shocked to see a gawker float into his bank's main branch. His shock only grew when two knights walked in and he realized one was Lady Thistle.

"Mr. Pennsburg, you looked a little shocked. Didn't expect to see me alive?"

"I have no idea what you are speaking of," he said.

"Perhaps all that leather has cut off the circulation to your brain and has made you forgetful."

"Have you come to protect me from these horrid bank robberies?" Pennsburg asked, taking out a hanky to dab at his forehead.

"Actually, we have come to arrest you for them," Sir Bult said.

"Why would you arrest an innocent man?" Abercrombie asked.

"We wouldn't," Thistle said. "You see, I recognized you."

"Well, my picture is in the paper often, especially on the social pages."

"No, I recognize you from your fall off the dragon."

"What a fanciful tale you weave, lady knight, but I have people who will swear that I was with them when this occurred."

"But she hasn't told you when it happened," Bult pointed out.

The banker shrugged. "It doesn't matter; I am rarely ever alone. Now if you'll excuse me, I wish to be about my business."

Bult grabbed him by the arm and lifted up his chin. "Nice bruise you have there."

"Ah yes. I was playing a game of cricket and my foot got stuck in a sticky wicket which made me fall. Very clumsy of me, but that's hardly a crime."

"Nice lie. The bruise is from where I hit you," Bult said.

"Says you. And your partner's claims that she saw my face is just her word against mine."

Bult leaned forward toward the man. "Knights of the Steam Table are not permitted to lie."

Abercrombie laughed. "And of course, no knight has ever lied."

The senior knight gritted his teeth but kept his cool. "You are under arrest."

"Then I invoke Noble Privilege."

"There is no record of you being a noble," Bult said.

"It seems the Duke of Pearl was having some financial difficulties and was about to go to prison for not paying some debts to his fellow nobles and the Crown. I simply offered him enough to pay them off and allowed him to keep his lands in exchange for the title. I have been a full-fledged duke for three days now. And as you know, that entitles me to a trial by the Queen. And I'm sure Her Majesty will see that this is just some horrible misunderstanding."

The way Bult broke into laughter and then began to choke at what the banker had conceived as a way around arrest confused Pennsburg, as did the gawker hovering directly in front of his face. "Very well, *Your Grace*, if that is what you wish then you shall have it. May God have mercy on your soul."

"Allow me to grab my cane and we'll be on our way," Pennsburg said, reaching out for the walking stick.

It was plucked from his grasp by Bult. "Sorry, Duke, but that is what is called evidence, not to mention common sense. If you think we are going to let you simply pick up a weapon, you are a fool."

Pennsburg managed to scowl and look down his nose at the knight simultaneously. The knights escorted the banker to the palace.

"I assume we are here just to make an appointment for the trial. It is my understanding that it takes two or three months for an audience with the Queen. Can I assume you'll let me out on bail until then?"

Bult laughed again while Thistle went skipping off down the corridor, returning mere moments later. "The Queen will see us now."

Pennsburg's jaw dropped. "Just like that? I have never heard of such a thing. Why I haven't even had time to engage a lawyer."

"You're confusing this with a trial. For Noble Privilege, you must speak for yourself," Bult said, shoving Pennsburg toward the door. "Let's go, Duke. Remember you have nobody to blame for this but yourself."

The Queen's Hall began to fill. Those in attendance were mainly staff whose jobs involved matters of Court since it was not a scheduled meeting. A man in red and black with a four-pointed hat and a staff with a carved head that wore a matching hat entered the room. He danced over to where the knights and the banker stood. The jester embraced the lady knight kissing her atop the forehead. "Hello, Thistle."

The lady knight hugged the man. "Hello, Daddy."

"Ah, her father is the jester. So that's how this happened so quickly."

"Not hardly," Bult said.

Trumpets sounded and all in the room went down on their right knee except Thistle. Pennsburg looked up and saw her insolence—Thistle had not genuflected, only bowed. The robber banker smiled to himself thinking that such a show of disrespect would surely have the Queen more disposed to hear his side of things. After all, he had just donated one hundred thousand pounds to her latest pet project. That should buy some leniency, even from Queen Theodora,

But there was no outcry from the Queen demanding that

she be forced to her knee. Instead, Her Majesty said, "Hello, Thistle."

"Hello, Auntie."

The color drained from Pennsburg's face. "Auntie?"

"Yes, my mother is the Queen's sister."

"And my niece is fifth in line for the throne," Queen Theodora said, the elfin queen taking her throne.

The jester skipped over and bonked Pennsburg on the head with his stick. "Underestimate my daughter? That'll teach you."

"Gomez, that is enough. After all, this man is now a duke."

"And I'm a prince," the jester said. "I outrank him."

"You are a prince consort. And you do outrank him. Regardless, do not hit the man," the queen ordered. The jester faked another swing which made Pennsburg flinch. The jester smiled and skipped away.

"Let's get on with this. What are the charges brought against the Duke of Pearl?"

Thistle cited the multiple laws that had been broken by the man in leather. "And during an attempted apprehension I managed to unmask the robber. It was Abercrombie Pennsburg."

"And how does the Duke of Pearl respond to these charges?" the Queen asked.

"Innocent on all counts, Your Majesty."

"Are you calling my niece a liar?" Queen Theodora inquired, frowning.

"Absolutely not, Your Majesty. I think it is simply a case of mistaken identity. I can provide witnesses, many witnesses in fact, to collaborate that I was elsewhere at the time of this robbery."

"Princess Thistle …"

"Your Majesty, I'm working," Thistle whispered.

The Queen sighed. "Lady Thistle, can anyone besides yourself collaborate your testimony?"

"Yes, I do have another witness."

"That's impossible! No one else was…" Pennsburg realized

silence was a better refuge than speaking and tried to fix his error in judgment. "Not that I would have any knowledge of those present since I myself was not."

"Knight, bring your witness forward."

"Your Majesty, I think it would be easiest if we stepped into the courtyard for this witness."

"Very well."

Queen Theodora clapped her hands twice and footmen rushed to open up the courtyard doors. After the Queen went through, the rest of the assembled filed out. When Pennsburg saw the giz dragon waiting there he tried to make a run for it. Bult was ready for him, his leg tripping Pennsburg. The knight reached down and yanked the man to his feet with a "My apologies, Your Grace."

Suffice it to say, Abercrombie Pennsburg's first royal audience with the Queen did not go as planned.

Despite his size, Samat made a very fine genuflection before stating, "Your Majesty, that is the man who fitted me with a necklace made of explosives and forced me to rob banks with him."

"That creature murdered two men and hospitalized others. Surely you are not going to take its word over that of a Duke?" Pennsburg said.

"Ah, but it is not just the giz, but my niece who has identified you."

"Your Majesty, I have recently donated one hundred thousand pounds to your favorite charity and have plans for an even more generous donation once this matter is resolved."

"Excellent. In recognition of your generosity…" Pennsburg smirked at Thistle and Bult, thinking he was about to be pardoned. "I will not sentence you to death. Instead, Abercrombie Pennsburg, Duke of Pearl, you are sentenced to life in Thames Tower. All your lands, title, and property are hereby seized by the Crown."

"What!? You can't do this to me! I'm rich. I'm a duke!"

"Were rich," Thistle said.

"Were a duke," Bult added.

Pennsburg was dragged away, screaming that he would have his revenge.

"Auntie, do you think you could grant Samat a private audience?"

"Isn't one request for an audience in a day enough, Niece? And who is Samat?"

"I am, Your Majesty," the mechanical dragon answered.

The Queen raised her eyebrows, then stroked her chin. "I suppose. Clear the courtyard."

With the exception of the two knights and a few of the Queen's retainers, they were alone in less than a minute.

The Queen, Thistle, and the giz walked and talked away from the rest at the far end of the courtyard. The Queen soon motioned for her niece to leave, so she skipped back to stand beside Sir Bult. At its finish, the gizzard bowed and took off into the sky.

"What! The giz is being allowed to leave!?" Sir Bult whispered in a tone that made it sound like a quiet scream.

Thistle motioned for her partner to follow, knowing the shame it would cause the knight should the queen notice his outburst, even as quiet as it was.

"Samat made a deal with Auntie. He knows where most of the stolen goods are kept. In exchange for returning them to the Crown, he is being given a full pardon and granted Pennsburg's title and some land far away in the mountains. It is inhospitable for farming or shepherding, but perfect for a giz looking for peace."

The knight cop growled. "Giz were the enemy. Samat was a thief and killed two men. He is too dangerous to let live, let alone be made one of the nobility."

"It is a sizable amount of money that otherwise will likely go forever unfound," Thistle said.

"Give me an hour alone with Pennsburg and we'll know where it is," Bult said.

Thistle simply smiled. "You haven't even heard the best part."

A sharp inhalation escaped Bult's lips as he saw the gawker

move in for a close-up. "What else?"

"As nobility, Samat must perform service for the Crown and Auntie has assigned him to the Steam Table, specifically us, to use as we see fit," Thistle said, then skipped away, leaving her partner silently clenching his fists so hard his fingers became pale.

Sir Bult then sighed and followed after his junior partner.

Jackson Grimstone, the Spellpunk

in

THAT VOODOO THAT YOU DO

"You have been found guilty of witchcraft. Before this court passes sentence, is there anything you would like to say?"

"May your manhood shrivel up and fall off," spat the girl, undeterred by the esteemed judge in front of her and the iron chains that bound her wrists and ankles. "All this because I wouldn't dab it up with you, you fat, cankerous blob of human waste."

Judge Kraz's taking advantage of female accused had evolved into something of a legend. Acquiescing to his demands was the easiest way to avoid trial, although it has been whispered that after allowing his perversions, more than one lass had said she would have preferred a conviction.

Kraz cringed. To be the subject of rumors was one thing, but to be accused in open court with reporters present was another. Especially by a girl who was barely into pubescence— her tender age could sway sympathy from any reporters who had daughters of their own. The situation had to be nipped in the bud.

"Your crimes weren't enough, so you have to try to besmirch a good man's name with these vile accusations."

"What good man? I was speaking of you."

"Bailiff, silence her. There shall be no mercy after these terrible lies. Make peace with your heathen gods because on the morrow you shall be hanged until dead."

"I object," said a voice from the back of the courtroom. The spectators turned to see a figure standing in the shadows.

"Objections are only for barristers during the trial, not sentencing. Another word and I will hold the speaker in contempt," Kraz yelled, pounding his gavel.

"I hold this entire proceeding in contempt and find the girl not guilty on account of…" The man paused and stroked his bare chin, trying to think of an answer. "Because I say so."

Kraz rose to his feet, knocking his horsehair wig back on his head. His face darkened and spittle flew from his lips as he said, "I will have that man in irons."

There was laughter as the man stepped forward and leaned on an ornately carved black cane topped with a metal handle that resembled the head of a dragon. He was clad in black, from the tails on his coat to the brimmed hat on his hairless head. The cane seemed more an affection than a need.

"Jackson Grimstone," Kraz spat out the name as if it was a curse. The judge lowered himself back into his chair. The crowd was soon abuzz with whispers of what the people called him. *Spellpunk.*

"Ah, Krazy, you remember me. I'm touched. Not as much as you," Grimstone said, "or young girls accused of witchcraft, apparently."

"This is my courtroom and I shalln't…."

"You shalln't interrupt the big people when they are speaking." Grimstone lifted his goggles and met the judge's eyes. "I believe I told you I did not want to see another of these circuses."

"But Ingeline Gray has been found guilty of witchcraft."

"By who? You? I laugh. Ha."

"She consorts naked with the Devil."

"Well, you can't very well consort fully clothed. It takes all the fun out of it. Although in your case, it might be considered mandatory to prevent screams of fear and a lifetime of nightmares." The Spellpunk punctuated his words with a smile, playing to the crowd, which rewarded him with laughter. Kraz, in turn, burned with anger.

Flipping the tip of the cane atop his right shoulder, Grimstone walked to the girl in chains.

"Tell me, girl, have you consorted with the Devil?"

"I have not."

"And has anyone asked you to become naked?"

"Him!"

Grimstone slowly turned his head, stopping in mock shock when his line of sight reached the judge. "Let the record show, she has indicted Krazy. So if she was asked to consort with you and she consorted with the Devil, I suppose we have no choice but to conclude that you are the Devil. How do you plead?"

"I object!"

Grimstone walked around the girl, dragging his cane tip along the floor as he went. "Pity, because as you so aptly pointed out, this is your court and objections are only for barristers during the trial, not sentencing. As you are the judge, I fear you hardly qualify. Sadly, I already held you in contempt and that was before I realized you were the Devil."

"Bailiffs, take this man into custody!"

"Really? You are going to take that tactic?" Grimstone rolled his eyes and looked at Ingeline. "Sad really, but what are you going to do?"

"I was working on escaping," the girl said.

Grimstone laughed. "Excellent. What was your plan?"

"Getting out of the chains and running far away, really quickly."

"Hmm…" Grimstone rubbed his chin. "Simple, understated. I like it. Mind if I help?"

"Not at all. Please feel free."

Grimstone pointed his cane, pushed the dragon's left eye and a knife blade popped out. He put it in the chain's padlock and twisted. The shackle popped open. The girl pulled the padlock off and her chains drizzled to the floor.

The bailiffs nervously stepped forward. Grimstone looked at them and the joking stopped as he pushed the blade back up in his cane.

"You do not want to do this."

"His Honor there thinks this is his courtroom, but it's not.

It's mine and no riff-raff is going to come in here and disrupt it," the head bailiff said.

"Then why pray tell do you let Krazy in day after day?"

The head bailiff pulled his flintlock pistol and aimed it at Grimstone's face. The Spellpunk swung his cane and knocked the gun to the side as the guard fired into a wall instead of his hide. Not for the first time, Grimstone was thankful the Bugeye's made the change to the steampunk motif and only introduced flintlock pistols instead of revolvers to the general populace. He only needed to avoid being shot once, instead of six or more times. As near as he could figure, the Bugeyes did it to keep the deaths–and the cost of introducing replacement people–down. Other playworlds like Doomstone and Konundrum City weren't so lucky.

"You pull a gun on me?" Grimstone punched the head bailiff in the jaw, threw a grappling hook over the arm of a statue of lady justice, hooked it to the man's belt, and pulled on the rope so the head bailiff dangled eight feet off the ground. Grimstone tied it off and laughed.

"When I get down from here…"

"What makes you think you're getting down?" Grimstone swung his cane at the court officer, purposely missing, but still close enough to make the man flinch. "I always loved a piñata."

"What's a piñata?" asked one of the pair of remaining bailiffs.

Grimstone rolled his eyes and shook his head. "Oh, for someone from Earth who would understand my best lines. So, gentlemen, I suggest surrender or retreat."

The two bailiffs looked from Grimstone to each other as he went back to stand next to the girl.

"You are surrendering to us?"

"Hardly. I was suggesting it to you. No? Fine. You have no one to blame but yourselves for what happens." The Spellpunk blew onto the palm of his hand and a small fireball lifted off and floated to the floor. An instant after contact, a circle of fire appeared in the path he had traced with his cane. Grimstone and the girl were inside, the rest of the court outside.

"Bye-bye." Grimstone snapped his fingers and the circle filled with smoke. Once it cleared, the man and the girl were gone.

"Grimstone!" screamed Kraz.

The girl looked up to the circular smoke-filled hole above them, then at the piece of floor beneath their feet, and realized Grimstone had somehow cut through the floor itself. "Why didn't that hurt when we landed?"

"I moved some of the mats from the cells to cushion our fall, but now is not the time for idle chit or chat. It is time for that running far away that you mentioned. Of course, we can chat as we flee if you like," said Grimstone, briskly jogging down a tunnel. "We can play follow the leader and hope the bailiffs are not very good at the game. This way, please."

Ingeline shucked off the last of her chains and followed after the man with the top hat and cane.

"Did you know they keep a dragon down here to eat escaping prisoners?" Grimstone said.

"I had heard that there was a giant mechanical giz down here left from the Zigat War. Is it true?" Ingeline asked.

"Don't know. Never seen it. Best not to dawdle, though," Grimstone said, leading the way through twists and turns of the underground maze.

"How can you tell where we are?"

"I know this place like the back of my hand," Grimstone said, holding up and wiggling his fingers.

"You're looking at the front of your hand."

"Then I guess we might be in for some trouble. No, wait, here we are," Grimstone said, as they stopped at the opening to a water drainage tunnel, but the term opening was somewhat misrepresentative as iron bars ran vertically into the cement.

"Bugger it. I'm smaller than you and I'm not going to fit through there," Ingeline said.

"And if you could, would you abscond, leaving me behind?" Grimstone asked, pulling at the cement and removing a sizeable brick block, which in turn left a gap large enough that the girl might slip through.

Ingeline looked at the opening, then at Grimstone who had taken his hat off and held it in front of his chest in what he hoped was a pitiable sight. She then turned back toward the sounds of their pursuers. The bailiffs were right on their trail, so recapture was only a matter of time. "Damn it, no. I want to, but it wouldn't be right. What are we going to do now?"

Grimstone smiled and used his dragon cane to put his top hat back on his head. "Oh, ye of little faith. Iron bars do not a prison make, although I'm told they are a crucial part of the setup. I'm Jackson Grimstone. Do you think a few bars are going to stop me?"

"Those are iron bars. Magic and iron don't mix well."

"Well, there is magic, and then there's *magic*." Grimstone started turning another of the iron bars and as he did so, it sunk into the lower part of the tunnel opening, which allowed him to bend it forward and pull it out. Between the removed bar and missing brick, there was enough room for both to go through. He bowed and motioned with his arm. "After you."

The sounds of the court officers got louder, so Ingeline rushed through. Grimstone followed, stopping to screw the bar back in and replace the cement brick.

"Exactly how did you know that was there?" she asked.

"I installed it the first time I had to get into the courthouse without anyone knowing how I did it," Grimstone said. "And I saw no reason to get rid of it. I hope I can trust your discretion."

"I'm not likely to tell anyone, but it just doesn't seem overly magical. Word on the street is you're more powerful than the Steam Table's master gearers and all I've seen you do so far are tricks," she said.

"There's your first lesson. Everything is a trick. Some are better than others, especially if the other guy doesn't know how you do it. From what I hear you have some very strong natural talent, but with all the folks flinging around claims of magic from the Steam Table Knights on down, it is highly unusual to be charged with witchcraft, so I am guessing you offended someone besides Judge Krazy back there. Watch that brown patch," Grimstone said, stepping around a rather fragrant pile of something he felt best remained unnamed before continuing his slosh through the pipe.

"I was trying to stop Baron Zambone."

Grimstone furrowed his brow. "I fancy myself familiar with all the nobility and I've not heard of a Baron Zambone."

"He is not a noble. He is a Voodoo practitioner."

Grimstone's eyebrows shot up. "Ah, that explains it. Let me guess, he is a dark-skinned man from the islands who wears a black outfit including a jacket but no shirt, a top hat, and has perhaps a skull tattooed or painted upon his face."

"Yes, you know him?"

"No, but I know how the Steamworld works. Playworlds like archetypes and it sounds like Baron Zambone is your stereotypical evil houngan."

"I don't understand. You talk about it like this is not your world."

"It's not. This world is a playworld, constructed and built for the entertainment of the Bugeyes, a race the universe would be much better off without. Or at least would have been better served if they had just stayed home and not bothered the rest of us. Their great obsession is the literary and pop culture of my native world and the fools have made entire planets just to indulge their appetite for entertainment."

A whooshing sound echoed through the tunnels as a flying metal sphere came out of the dark to hover near them. "Speak of the bug-eyed devils and their spy cameras appear. The gawkers are their eyes and ears for broadcasts back home." Grimstone took a swipe with his cane at the floating camera, but it pulled back at the last minute, avoiding the blow.

"Why is it here?"

"Obviously, something bad is about to happen to us that it wants to record for posterity. However, it can record my posterior." Grimstone lowered his pants and wagged his rear at the gawker. The floating camera focused in and Grimstone then returned his pants to the full and upright position. "They are, however, a decent early warning system, so keep your eyes open."

"The rumors of other worlds are true?" Ingeline asked. Grimstone nodded. "I'm orphaned and never knew my parents. The tales say that many of the people on this world were stolen from elsewhere and brought here. I have always fancied myself as one of them."

"You may very well be. I was taken from Earth, my home world, against my will. I wasn't the only one they took. The bastards separated me from my four-year-old daughter. I have been searching the playworlds for her ever since. I learned they brought her here and I won't leave until I find her."

The girl's eyes lit up. "How long ago was that?"

Grimstone's face turned dark. "Almost five years."

The girl's face looked crestfallen. "Oh."

The odd reaction did not go unnoticed by the Spellpunk. "What's the matter?"

"I guess I was hoping that perhaps... I might be your daughter. I never knew my parents, so I thought maybe I was the one you were looking for, but I'm thirteen, not nine. I guess no one cared enough to look for me."

Grimstone became very still and placed his hand tenderly on the girl's shoulder. "Don't think like that. I have been very fortunate in that I figured out a way to travel between the playworlds. I am one of the few who has managed it. Just because no one has come looking, doesn't mean they don't miss you and haven't tried."

The girl nodded and stopped, staring straight ahead. Grimstone turned in the same direction. At the end of the tunnel sloshing through the muck and mire was a trio of rats, each the size of a Great Dane.

"The gawker early-warning system strikes again," Grimstone said. "There is something you don't see every day,"

"The giant rats?" said the girl.

"No, three of them working in unison. Rats of that size are not pack-minded animals. They get very territorial and are more likely to fight than work with each other. I'm going to guess we have another visitor riding along. Isn't that right, Baron Zamboni?"

The center rat's eyes glowed in the blackness and a sound something like a human voice escaped the rat's throat. "Very good, Grimstone. I have heard of you and it appears that some of your reputation may be deserved after all."

"I've heard of you too, although not until just a couple of minutes ago. And I'm wondering about the name, why would you name yourself after a Zamboni? Are there a lot of ponds that need the ice smoothed out? I wasn't aware that the city Thames even had ice hockey or figure skating."

"What the blazes are you talking about?" the rat said.

Grimstone shrugged. "Sometimes it would be nice to meet somebody new from back home, even if it was an adversary. I'm sure, Zamboni, that you know you are blocking our escape. Get your rodents to move aside and we'll be on our way, please and thank you."

The rat laughed. The sound and action were both chilling and made the girl shiver. "I have no problems with you, Grimstone, but the girl has crossed me. I cannot allow that to go unpunished. You are said to have a similar code allowing no one who crosses you to go unpunished."

"In some ways, perhaps. But where do you get off trying to kill a girl? What exactly did she do that is so deserving of death?"

"She tried to turn the children against me," the rat answered.

Grimstone hesitated for a moment, a different vision of the houngan entering his mind and for an instant saw him through a father's eyes. "Are you talking about your children?"

The rat chuckled, the noise like nails on a chalkboard and the wail of a dying cat. "Of course not. I'm speaking of the street urchins who do my business. That witch tried to get them to rebel."

"I see," Grimstone said, his eyes turning to the girl. "Give me your version, but make it quick."

"I grew up on the streets. Sometimes kids have to do things they don't want to do, mostly stealing. There is usually a fee paid to gangs in that neighborhood for the rights, but Zambone has forced many of the kids to work solely for him. They have no freedom, he controls every aspect of their lives, and much of what he makes them do is far worse than stealing. I tried to put an end to it. I did pretty good too."

"If you call freeing a dozen children out of a hundred good, then yes," the rat said. "I would call it more of a petty annoyance. It's the principle of the thing. I can't be seen as weak. All I need is the head, Grimstone. You can have the rest of her."

"I think we'll keep her intact. Ingeline, were there many eight or nine-year-old girls involved?"

Ingeline nodded. "About seven, I think."

Grimstone nodded and pointed his cane at the center rat. The floating gawker moved in for a close-up. "Zamboni, I am serving you notice. This girl is under my protection, as are all the other children. You will quite simply not bother them again. I shall arrange for their egress from your dark service, all at no cost to you. I trust we have an agreement?"

"Those children have helped make me wealthy and will continue to do so. You're quite mad if you think I am going to do anything but continue to have them fatten my pockets."

"Very well. A shame we couldn't have done this the easy way. Consider this your notice. I'm coming for you, Zamboni."

The rat laughed again and this time pulled out all the stops, sounding like thunder filtered through the mouth of a screaming child.

"Zamboni, I have no idea just how to tell you this, but rats were not meant to laugh. It's not scary or frightening; it's just sad and pathetic."

"What's sad and pathetic is that you believe you are going to survive long enough to get past my pets and out of this tunnel."

"Your funeral, Zamboni. I'll be seeing you soon," Grimstone said, bringing the bottom of his cane even with the rat's head. He pressed a scale on the dragon handle, which caused a loud noise. Smoke belched out of the bottom as the talking rat's head exploded in a meaty and bloody mess.

The rat on the right advanced on the girl, while the one on the left decided to hunt Grimstone.

The girl backed away slowly. "Now, if you could just blow up the heads of the other two, we can be on our way. And if it could be done quickly, it would be appreciated."

"No can do. The cane only holds one shot. But you are a convicted witch. Surely you can use some witchy wiles to take care of at least one of these foul creatures?"

"I can summon light," the girl said sheepishly.

"Bringing light to the darkness of this world is a noble skill, but not overly good for offensive maneuvers. Do you have any other psychic powers that could help us?"

"Psychic? What are you talking about? Tis magic."

"Tomato, to-mot-toe. Magic, pyscholuminescence. Let's not worry about the words when we should be worried about living. Fortunately, I have one or two more other tricks left." With that, Grimstone pulled his cane back and swung at the gawker, thrusting it at the closest rat. The gawker righted itself before making impact, but did distract the beast.

"I'll show you and I'll take care of this one myself," said the girl. She waved her hand and said, "*Luminous!*" Light burst from her hand, blinding the rat.

Ignoring his own safety by not dealing with the now-aggravated giant rodent nearest him, Grimstone pointed the mouth of his dragon handle at the blinded rat attacking the girl and twisted the shaft. Fire belched out from the dragon handle mouth, setting the giant beast aflame.

The gawker moved in a full circle around the burning freak of laboratory science and magic as the creature rushed further down the tunnel in a vain attempt to outrun the hungry flames licking at its flesh.

The third rat beast seemed brighter than the other two and had backed away to contemplate its next move.

"Can't you cook this one or is the fire another one-trick-wonder?" asked the girl.

"It's not, but I hate to repeat myself. Where I come from, we have a saying, 'a good magician doesn't perform the same trick twice in a row'," Grimstone said.

The rat beast growled at them and the gawker floated down

to get a better angle for the shot for the bug-eyed viewers. Grimstone smiled, then swung the cane like a sword at the floating sphere and did it twice more, knocking the gawker down the gullet of the giant rodent. Grimstone stepped forward and wrestled so his arms were around the mouth of the rat beast and squeezed it closed.

The tremendous rodent reacted by shaking its head, the movement lifting Grimstone off the ground, but the Spellpunk did not let go even though every flick of the rat's neck tossed him around like a rag doll. The rat couldn't dislodge him, but did make the Spellpunk drop his cane. The front of the rodent's throat began to rise, then bulge until finally, the gawker burst out through flesh and trachea.

The beast tried to roar again, but it came out a gurgle. Grimstone held on as the beast convulsed and wrestled it to the ground, not letting go until it moved no more.

"Damn, you are good," the girl said.

Grimstone stood up, wiping the blood from his hands onto the dead rodent's hide, then took a bow. "Thank you."

"You're either braver or more foolish than I have even heard to mistreat a gawker like that." The gawker plunged into the murky water of the sewer in an attempt to clean itself, then rose out and spun itself dry, but wetting Grimstone. "That's one of the few crimes that the Crown prosecutes against almost anyone, even nobility."

"In this case, I don't think the Bugeyes will mind. I'm sure they got some good shots from inside the creature as they burst out."

"I don't understand what you are saying," the girl said.

"Never mind, it's not important. Let's get you to my house so I can figure out what I'm going to do against Zamboni."

"What *we* are going to do," she corrected. Grimstone raised an eyebrow. "I started this. If you think I'm not going to finish it, you are sorely mistaken."

The Spellpunk rubbed his chin, fighting back a smile. "So you are willing to risk your hide to rescue those children?"

"Absolutely. Nobody was there for me when I needed it, so

I'm going to make damn well sure that's not going to happen to those kids."

"Excellent answer."

A while and several underground twists and turns later, Grimstone removed a grate and the pair climbed up to street level in a deserted alley. Grimstone motioned the girl to follow him and they went onto the street and up a flight of stairs that lead to the biggest residence Ingeline had ever been that close to while not trying to steal anything.

Grimstone lifted the dragon-shaped knocker and banged on the heavy wooden door.

"I thought you said we were going to your house," Ingeline said.

"This is my house," Grimstone said.

"It's more of a mansion actually, but if it's yours, why are you knocking?"

"I don't want to startle my butler," he replied.

"Why would you be worried about startling your butler? After all, he works for you…."

The door opened and the sight that greeted her stopped Ingeline mid-sentence. A seven-foot-tall green man with pointed ears and sharp teeth looked down at her.

"Your butler is a troll!"

In response, the green man narrowed his brows and frowned. Ingeline took a step back.

"Yes, Smithers is, but trolls are actually just humans the Bugeyes mutated for their own purposes. Same as the royal family being elves. Just a dominant trait for pointy ears. Otherwise, they and the elf commoners are as human as the rest of us. One of the times the genetic code turned out stable enough for breeding," Grimstone said. "Unlike the poor Hoodoo who were the dominant native life form here before the Bugeyes moved the humans in."

"Honestly, sometimes it's like you are speaking another language," Ingeline said. "Does he bite?"

"Yes, Miss," Smithers replied. "But you have to ask very nicely."

"And if I ask you nicely not to?"

"Hmm, that depends."

"On what?"

"Jackson, is the lady friend, foe, or other?" the troll asked.

Grimstone hid a smile. "I'm leaning toward friend at the moment."

"Excellent. Very well then, Miss, no biting," Smithers said, motioning them inside. "For now."

"Um, thank you, I guess," she said.

"My pleasure. Now, what have you gotten involved in that puts you in Mr. Grimstone's company and makes you smell that badly? And have another of these gawkers following you about." The troll tried to close the door, but the flying camera slipped in before the wood met the jam.

Grimstone summarized.

"I've never been fond of Judge Kraz myself. Been before him twice myself. I was found not guilty the first time," Smithers said.

"And the second time?" asked Ingeline.

The green behemoth grinned.

"Let's just say Smithers was not always the gentleman's gentleman you see before you today," said Grimstone.

"No, I was not," said Smithers. "I'm afraid I reacted a bit barbarically. I may have threatened the judge. And tore apart the court."

"Really? What happened?" Ingeline asked.

"Krazy soiled himself and doubled the sentence," Grimstone said. "And the first sentence was life."

"Then how did you get out?" Ingeline asked.

"It was thanks to Mr. Grimstone here, who oddly enough, was my sworn enemy."

"Only because you twice tried to kill me," said Grimstone. "Before the bet."

"Three times, actually. Suffice it to say, the third time was not the charm, but was far enough off that you were unaware," Smithers said.

Grimstone raised an eyebrow. "Really? We'll have to talk

more about that later, but suffice it to say, I made a deal for Smithers's freedom."

"What kind of deal?"

"He bet the queen he couldn't turn me into a polite manservant within a month. Considering our history, it was a bet Queen Theodora thought she could win," Smithers said.

"You bet the queen?"

Grimstone shrugged. "Most are too intimidated and of those that do, many throw the bet in an attempt to weasel their way into Teddie's good graces."

"The queen lets you call her Teddie?"

"Lets?"

"Ignore him, Miss," Smithers said. "He has done much for the queen and does not put her up on a pedestal."

"Well, just the one time, but she had me tossed in a cell for looking up her skirt," Grimstone said.

"Her Majesty enjoys the company of one who is honest, almost always to a fault, and who is not intimidated by her," the troll said. "He does tend to use it to his advantage."

"I didn't hear you complaining when it got you out of prison."

"No, the bet was a good thing," Smithers replied.

"I take it Her Majesty lost?" Ingeline said.

"Sadly. In fact, Krazy himself told me he would commute my sentence to time served if I killed Mr. Grimstone for him. Even gave it to me in writing."

"Which is how I can get away with disrupting his court. We still have the signed document with his personal seal," Grimstone said.

"For blackmail purposes and just in case you do get killed." The Spellpunk turned and glared at the troll manservant. "By someone other than me, of course. I haven't tried to kill you in ages."

"No, you just lie in wait to attack me," Grimstone said.

"At your request, and I quote, 'To prevent you from getting sloppy'."

"I get sloppy, I get dead, right?"

"Which is why I have the document. When..." Another glare from the Spellpunk. "... I mean, *if* you die, I plan to take the credit and gain my freedom."

Grimstone smiled.

"So you have stopped trying to kill him?" Ingeline asked.

"Sadly. Jackson Grimstone is a good man, a rarity in any race. Being addressed as Smithers is bad enough, but when I attack him, he calls me Cato and I do wish he would stop."

Grimstone chuckled. "Trust me, where I'm from it's hilarious and would make perfect sense."

The Spellpunk turned and looked at the gawker. "Wouldn't it, Bugeyes? Anyway, Smithers is my personal Eliza Doolittle."

"Grimstone, you are losing me again," Ingeline said.

"Miss, I too do not understand him when he speaks like that, if that is any consolation," Smithers said. "Allow me to fetch both of you some dry and less fragrant clothing. Perhaps draw you each a bath?"

"No time for the bath. Just bring the clothes, please."

Ingeline scowled as she looked from one male to the other, her hands on her hips. "We are covered in sewer filth. I am not going anywhere until I am clean. And I will not smell you the whole time, so you will clean up at well."

"We can shower first then," Grimstone said, trying to hide a grin from the way he was being ordered about.

"Excuse me?" she said, suddenly indignant. "We?"

"There are five separate bathrooms in this building. The nearest one for Miss is down the main hall," Smithers said.

"They had *better* be separate," she said.

"You are still a child. I know others may not make that distinction, but I do. I am not like Krazy. My statement was not an attempt to solicit something sorted," Grimstone said. "I am not a bad man."

"At least not when it comes to children," Smithers reluctantly conceded.

A short time later, the pair were clean and in fresh clothes.

"So, Sir, off to squash Baron Zambone?" Smithers asked.

"Yes, but I thought perhaps you might like to join us,"

Grimstone said.

"My duties are limited to the house as per our agreement. Why would I want to help you on one of your fool's quests?"

"Did I mention Zamboni's captives are children?"

"You most surely did not," Smithers said. "Allow me to get my hat and coat and I will join you." The troll walked at a brisk pace down the hall.

"He has a soft spot for kids?" Ingeline asked.

Grimstone nodded. "He's a father. In fact, he stopped trying to kill me the day I saved his daughter."

"You saved a troll?"

"Quite a few, actually."

"Hmm. Perhaps you had an anterior motive, thinking that by saving her you might guilt the troll trying to kill you into stopping his homicidal attempts by putting him in your debt. Hardly a selfless act," Ingeline said.

"You might have a point had I ever told Smithers. We have never discussed it. In fact, while I am certain that he knows, I am still not sure how he found out, as I did not announce myself to the trolls, but that is neither here nor there. We have a houngan to vanquish," Grimstone said, leaving by the front door. "Coming, Smithers?"

"Just getting Betsy," came the troll's reply.

"Who is Betsy? A mechanical giz that does your housekeeping?" Ingeline said.

"No, this is Betsy," said the troll, re-entering the room with a top hat, long coat, and a club almost as large as the convicted witch.

"You are allowed to carry a weapon that large?" she asked.

"The Steam Table Knights frowned upon it until Grimstone pointed out that I was allowed, like any sentient, to carry a walking stick," the troll said, holding the wide end in the palm of his hand, the narrow end touching the floor. Smithers moved it with each stride he made. "Quite becoming, no?"

"It certainly is unique," she said.

Grimstone hailed a livery cab whose driver tried to take off once he caught sight of Smithers, but Grimstone grabbed hold of the horse's rein until the troll and girl had already boarded the cab.

Ingeline gave him the address. Grimstone had the driver stop a block away and the trio walked the rest of the way.

"That is the factory where he keeps the children," Ingeline said. "Do we sneak in?"

"If Zamboni is any good, and his control of those rats tells me he is, he already knows we're here. Let's use the front door. He might not be expecting it and if clients have to use it, it is less likely to be booby-trapped," Grimstone said.

"Why don't the little ones just walk out?" Smithers asked, despite himself, opening the door for the other two. Of course, as it was locked, he did have to yank rather hard and ended up separating it from its hinges.

"There's your answer," Grimstone said, his eyes looking inside. The Spellpunk gritted his teeth at the sight of the tiny corpse attached to the wall with railroad spikes like a butterfly in an entomologist's display box and ropes reinforcing the spikes. Ingeline gasped. Smithers's hands gripped the door so hard the wood cracked and splintered beneath the pressure of his fingers. "Sick bastard."

The gawker flew in for a close-up of the boy's corpse. "I stand corrected. Sick bastards." The Spellpunk whacked the floating sphere with his cane. It only floated back out of his reach.

Grimstone stepped up and pulled out the iron spikes from the dead child's arms and legs.

"And this is allowed to go on why?" Smithers asked, his arms trembling from the effort of not hitting something. Instead, he put the door down next to Betsy and moved forward to help the Spellpunk get the child down.

"This playworld is based on Victorian England. Lots of bad things happened to children. They were often considered property rather than people, so the mores come through."

Smithers pulled at the iron railroad spikes in the boy's legs. Grimstone gave up trying to untie the knots in the ropes on the child's arms and pulled a blade from his sleeve to slice through the ropes.

"I still do not completely believe your tales that this is a playworld," Smithers said, removing the last spike.

The gawker spun in the air to focus on Grimstone's reply. He ignored it and cut through the last of the bonds. "Then explain our little floating nuisance here."

"I cannot," said Smithers, taking the child's feet while Grimstone held the boy under the arms. The pair laid him gently on the ground. The Spellpunk reached out and closed the dead boy's eyelids.

"His name was Jim," Ingeline whispered through tears.

"Well, little Jim, you will be avenged," Grimstone said.

"I doubt it," said the corpse, his just-closed eyes popping back open. This time, the pupils glowed green like the lead rat's had.

"Zamboni," Grimstone spat.

"Very good. Although the name is Zambone," the possessed boy's corpse said, leaping to his feet, each of his hands grabbing hold of a throat of the men who had cut him down. "Now die."

Grimstone used his knife to cut through the wrist of the hand holding him. Smithers tore the arm off at the shoulder, but the effort made his face look like the troll was about to cry at the desecration.

"Zombie. How original. You can't possibly think this will stop us," Grimstone said, taking the hand from his throat and throwing it on the ground. It scurried away like a crab, leaving behind bleeding scratch lines on the Spellpunk's neck.

"I had hoped you'd be squeamish enough about hurting the boy that I'd be able to end you quickly, but I hadn't counted on it. Goodbye, Grimstone."

The glow from the dead boy's eyes spread through the head and then his entire body.

"Run!" Grimstone yelled, pushing the troll and the girl back toward the doorway they had come through, but it was too little too late. The young corpse exploded in a rain of eldritch energy mixed with bone and meaty bits. The troll butler moved to shield the girl and the explosion hit his back full force. The

Spellpunk likewise moved to put himself between the girl and harm's way. The force of the blast threw Smithers so his body struck Grimstone, smashing the Spellpunk into Ingeline, and knocking them all to the floor.

Mocking laughter rang out as the pair bled out onto the floor. "The legendary Spellpunk and his pet troll laid low by Baron Zambone. Truly a marvelous day. Now, missy, I can see you are alive under Grimstone. Crawl your way out of there and we shall conclude our business."

Zambone walked in, rhythmically swinging a machete blade side to side as if cutting through an invisible jungle. He was, just as Grimstone had predicted, shirtless with a black suit, hat, and a skull painted onto his face.

Ingeline squirmed out and away from the Baron. "So you can separate my head from my shoulders? I think not."

"Technically, I will be separating it from your neck, but if saying shoulders makes you happy, I won't steal what little joy you have left away from you." The Baron drew the blade across his left index finger, drawing blood, then licking it off. "But you have no one to blame for your death but yourself. You made me look foolish by taking those children from me, so I need to make an example. You could have let Judge Kraz do it for me, but no, you had to escape."

As if the words inspired her, Ingeline raced toward the door, which slammed shut before she reached it.

"No leaving before I get the decoration for my pike." Zambone raised the blade.

"*Luminous!*" Ingeline shouted and light shone from her hand in an attempt to blind Zambone.

"*Shadow!*" In much the same way as Ingeline's light, darkness shot out from the Baron's hand. The opposing energies met and canceled each other out.

Grimstone tried to do the same to Zambone by smashing the houngan on the head from behind with his dragon cane. The Baron staggered forward and Grimstone used the cane to sweep the houngan's legs out from under him.

Grimstone stood above him, his cane aimed at Zombone's

head like it was a rifle. "Any last words, Zamboni?"

"Yes. Do not move."

Grimstone tried to laugh but found he was frozen to the spot.

Zambone pulled out what looked like a poor child's rag doll and held it up toward the Spellpunk. "I own you now, Grimstone."

Even bespelled and immobilized, the Spellpunk still managed to scowl.

"How did you…" Ingeline asked and was answered before she even finished by the houngan taking the dead boy's hand out of his pocket.

"Grimstone's blood was under the fingernails. It wasn't much, but enough for me to forever link him to my doll," Zambone said. "What do you think of that, *Spellpunk?*"

Grimstone did not respond.

"Oh my, very silly of me. You cannot speak unless I allow it. Very well, allow it I shall. You may talk, Grimstone."

"Nice trick, Zamboni, but it won't work for long. I don't believe in Voodoo," said Grimstone.

"Then why don't you come over here and hit me?" said Zambone.

The Spellpunk leapt forward, but the Baron held up the hand with the doll. "Stop. Most excellent reflexes. My own fault, really. Why don't you explain why your belief has anything to do with my control of you?"

The houngan walked over to the unconscious troll, sliced him with his machete then held a second doll to the wound until it was covered in Smithers' blood. The gawker moved in for a close-up and the Baron smiled for the floating sphere.

"Simple, Zamboni. What you call magic ties into a field which all living things give off. Anything with a person's genetic material will allow you to tie into their body. Hair and nails work, but are dead, so they don't work as well as blood."

"I don't know what genetic means, but otherwise, you have only explained how my magic works. What difference does your belief make?"

"Simple. I control my own life field so I can change the

frequency and leave you powerless," said Grimstone.

The Baron laughed. "It is possible I grant you, with months or years of concentration. You do not have that kind of time. Kraz failed me, so I think I will simply send you to kill him and then die yourself when the Steam Table Knights come for you. What do you think of that?"

"Not crazy about it. I say we go with Plan B."

"There is no Plan B," Zambone said as Ingeline rammed one of the iron spikes that held the boy to the wall into the Baron's rib cage.

"There is always a Plan B," Grimstone said.

Zambone spun, hitting the girl with his elbow, and knocking her down. He stumbled away from her. "Bitch!"

"Nasty chest wound there, Zamboni. Lots of sucking when you breathe. Not pretty," Grimstone said.

"Shut up and hit the girl," Zambone ordered.

Grimstone stepped forward and slapped Ingeline so hard she fell to the ground.

"Yes! You shall be the instrument of my destruction. Take my blade and use it to remove her head."

Grimstone turned stiffly, then held out his hand. The houngan placed the machete in the Spellpunk's palm.

"Thank you," Grimstone said.

"You are welcome," Zambone said. His pupils grew larger. "But I forbade you to speak."

"Yeah, I don't take orders so well," Grimstone said as he swung the blade. The blade sliced through a neck, but it wasn't Ingeline's. The Baron grabbed his throat in a vain attempt to stop his blood from flowing and spurting out, then fell to his knees as his efforts failed. Grimstone moved to take a second swing, then thought better of it and offered the machete to Ingeline.

The witch nodded, stood, then finished the decapitation Grimstone had begun with many swings. Her arms tired and her dress bloody, Ingeline tossed the blade aside.

"Thank you," she said.

"Think nothing of it."

"How did you break Zambone's spell? Surely not by belief alone."

"Nah. When he let me speak I made sure I bit and bloodied the inside of my mouth to help me focus and give me a starting point. He had a little blood, but I had a whole body full so I simply cast the same *spell* he did. Closer to quantum mechanics than magic."

"And you got back control of your body?"

"Not exactly, but I exerted enough control to be able to speak. That caused his belief in his own power to waver and I simply did as he told me, only changed the target."

"Hmm. Then I suppose I forgive you for hitting me," she said, rubbing her jaw. "What do we do next?"

"Wake up Smithers and stop his bleeding. He'll be in a foul mood since he missed everything, then we will go find the children and see if my daughter is among them."

"And the rest of the children?"

"In my quest to find my stolen child, I have freed many others so I fund an orphanage. A very good one. No mistreatment or they answer to me. These children will be well taken care of, taught to read and write, along with some basic science and engineering skills that will allow them to earn a living when they are older."

"You're not quite the bastard your reputation makes you out to be."

Grimstone smiled and picked the Baron's top hat off his separated head, then used it like a net to catch the gawker. Using the houngan's belt, he squeezed the opening of the felt hat into a sack and tied the end. The gawker was still able to fly, but not see where it was going. It flew and banged off the walls and ceiling, hopelessly lost.

"Oh, I am. I haven't told you the best part." Grimstone picked up the severed head. "I think we should pay Krazy a visit tonight and put Zamboni's head on the pillow next to him while he sleeps."

"Okay, you *are* a bastard, but I think I like you."

"Of course you do. You have excellent taste."

Lil Repute

in

Attack of the Body Patchers

The lightning made the hairs on the back of Lillian Repute's neck stand up. The last bolt was too close for her comfort, especially standing where she was. She stared at the lightning rod and wondered who in blazes was stupid enough to put a hunk of metal on their roof. Then she realized that someone who was standing on said roof in the middle of a thunderstorm wasn't exactly in the running for the clearest thinking woman in the city of Thames.

It would've been much simpler to simply knock on the front door, but far riskier. The Duchess Everlast was very powerful in both social and political circles. Although rumored to be more than ninety years old, her advanced years did not make her any less vengeful against those who crossed her.

To show up on her doorstep and inquire, however politely, if some missing prostitutes happened to be held prisoner somewhere in her mansion would likely not have elicited a positive response. Then if Duchess Everlast found out that not very long ago, Lil herself had been working the streets of Thames as a lady of the evening… well, it would likely have ended with the door being slammed into her face.

Many wives and widows viewed Lil, even now, with all that she had accomplished, with disdain and hatred simply upon learning about what she once did to survive. And were Lil to be reasonable, she would admit to understanding the impulse. After all, a great many of her former clients were themselves married men who weren't getting what they wanted or thought they needed at home, so they saw fit to seek fulfillment elsewhere. In her uncharitable moments, Lil would suggest the women get their own house in order before criticizing someone else's.

There weren't many folks who looked out for the lost women of Thames. Sure, there was the Spellpunk and a few of the Steam Table Knights, but there had to be more than one streetwalker killed before it even made the front page of the papers and the three missing women she sought were just that– missing. There were no bodies for the Knights to find or the reporters to write stories about. Even the Knights who cared assumed that the women had simply packed up and moved. But these women had skipped the packing up part and left all they owned.

Streetwalkers did not have much. It was part of why they did what they did. For three women to leave the entirety of their belongings behind seemed unlikely.

And it seemed far more than a coincidence that the last person who had spoken to all three women was described as a white-haired woman in her nineties. There were likely not a hundred women in the city who could fit that description, but January, one of the other prostitutes in the neighborhood, swore the woman was the Duchess Everlast and even recognized her signature peacock-headed cane. Jan's mother had been the Duchess's maid and she had lived in the Everlast Mansion up until her mother's death. The Duchess was not fond of children and simply put the twelve-year-old newly orphaned girl who was just blooming into womanhood out on the streets with nothing but the clothes on her back. And Jill had remained there ever since, as did her hatred for the woman who'd cast her off like so much human garbage.

It was possible that the Duchess simply preferred women to men now that she was a widow. It was not that unusual. The girls could have been taken in as part of the household staff or even as concubines and be perfectly safe and happy. If that were the case, Lil would be very pleased to walk away without ever having spoken to the Duchess. However, this seemed unlikely as the old woman had let go most of her household staff except for a few loyal retainers when she took the notorious Dr. Shelly into her home.

The man had a reputation for bizarre experiments involving grafting parts of one animal to another. There was talk that not all of his experiments had been on lower life forms. Shelly was rumored to be the one who had grafted a tiger's paw to Baron Rogan. Lil worried for the safety of the missing women and if she saw anything dark and depraved, would stop at nothing to get them out.

As Lil couldn't go in the front door, her options were limited. The Duchess Everlast had bars on all of her windows, even those on the second and third floors. That left the roof and a choice of four different chimneys, two of which had fires burning. Of the remaining pair, one was at the rear of the house in an area most likely to be devoid of people.

Lil hated chimneys. She didn't know how chimney sweeps did their jobs in such a dirty and confined space, especially with the risk of soot warts on their privates. She was fortunate to be slender enough to fit. Lil covered her eyes with goggles and her mouth and nose with a mask complete with filters. Using a knotted rope anchored around the chimney, Lil lowered herself down. When she emerged from the fireplace, she was covered in ash and soot. Reaching into a pouch at her waist, she pulled a cloth to clean the goggles and her face as best she could.

Lil crept through the big house, checking in each room and closet for the women. With the exception of a lot of dust and tarps covering the ridiculously expensive furniture, she found nothing. The three manservants the Duchess had were sound asleep and the remainder of the servants' quarters were empty. So much for the Duchess having hired on the women.

Not for the first time, Lil worried that she would not find them. Then she would have to take matters into our own hands and interrogate the old woman. She had a full head mask in the pouch in hopes of not being recognized. A commoner like her assaulting a high-ranking member of the aristocracy would likely end with her being topped and left dangling from the gallows after a speedy and public trial.

The rest of the house was empty. The Duchess's room had not been slept in. One of the guest quarters was made up but was also untouched. The Duchess' carriage and horses were still in her stable, so where were the woman and her guest?

Lil returned to the library. Something had struck her as odd about the room, so she went back to figure out exactly what that was.

By counting her paces in the room and in the corridor outside. Lil realized that the library should have been five paces larger than it was.

The library, like the rest of the house, was covered in dust, yet the floor was quite clean. One particular volume on the shelf showed finger marks. The title of the leather-bound book was *Electricity Is the Life* by someone named Victor Frankenstein. Lil reached up and pulled the volume out and was not surprised when the bookcase swung in like a door. She stepped inside, shut the bookcase, and headed down a stone staircase. Flickering gas lights lit her way.

Lil peeked around the corner at the bottom of the steps. A man in a long gray smock covered in red and gore was standing over a body and stitching it together. The butchered corpses of the three missing women lay on nearby tables and were missing parts—the legs and pelvis had been taken from one, the torso from another, and the arms from the third. The man had sewn them together and topped them off with the head and neck of an old, wrinkled woman who was undoubtedly the Duchess Everlast. A gawker floated above him.

Lil was too late to save the missing women, but she could still avenge them. She pulled out her flintlock pistol and pointed it at the man.

"Dr. Shelly, put down the needle and turn around slowly." Despite everything she'd been through, Lil still couldn't shoot an unarmed man in the back.

"Go away. This is a crucial junction for my work. I've just connected two spinal cords and now have to close the body before the storm leaves us."

Lil stepped closer. "I said put down the needle and turn around."

The mad doctor ignored her. "Jonathan, what did I make you for? Take care of the intruder."

From an alcove behind her, out stepped a monstrosity. It had the body and right arm of an ape, the head and left arm of a tiger, the legs of a man, and the tail of what appeared to be an alligator. Lil turned and fired, hitting the monstrosity in the chest. It twitched, then took the weapon from her hand with the tiger paw and the ape hand wrapped around her throat and squeezed until she faded into darkness.

In the deep darkness, Lil Repute dreamed of lightning flowing through wires into a corpse made of four women as Shelly danced around it and cackled, "It's reanimated!"

Her next thoughts were when she woke, chained to a metal table as naked as the days when she used to work indoors. Her hands were above her head and her ankles by the foot of the table. She tried to sit up and pull herself free but the chains held her fast.

A gawker floated down and hovered between her legs. Lil managed to smack it away by flexing her knee. It floated up to a corner. "Perverted Bugeyes!"

"It's about time you woke up. I've been quite bored waiting for some splendid conversation, you know."

She looked over to see a familiar man with a shaved head and a similar lack of clothing, chained down to a table identical to hers. "Grimstone? What are you doing here?"

"I came here to stop Shelly. Unfortunately, that monstrosity of his took me out first."

"It got me too."

Grimstone's face softened. "I have to admit I'm touched that you cared enough to come searching for me. Don't worry. I'll get us both out of this."

"I didn't come here looking for you. I was searching for the women Shelly butchered. And I'll get myself out of this, thank you very much."

Grimstone smiled as she struggled against the unyielding metal links. "Or we could work together."

Lil sighed. "Your suggestion does make a certain amount of sense. You've been here longer. What have you come up with?"

"Well, one thing has come up since you arrived, but I'm not sure how much help it'll be." The Spellpunk grinned and winked.

Lil glanced over and saw part of him standing at attention. "Really, Grimstone? A time like this and that's what you're thinking of?"

"It's not my fault. You're a very attractive and quite naked woman. I find myself thinking back to our last night together and it triggered a reflex. I apologize if my reaction gave you offense."

Despite herself, Lil smiled. "You can be an arrogant ass, but you're one of the few men I know who would apologize for that and not try to blame it on me for doing it to you."

"I come from a world obsessed with political correctness."

"What does that mean? You pick the correct politicians? When you talk about your so-called Earth, you make little sense."

"You are kind. Many people feel I make little sense most of the time."

They both fell silent as the door to their cell creaked open and in walked a wrinkled old woman, at least from the neck up. From the neck down, she had the body of a twenty-year-old. Three of them, in fact.

Yet she still walked with a peacock-headed cane.

A second gawker followed her in.

"Duchess Everlast, I must say for a wrinkly old hag, you're looking well." The patchwork woman wore a dress with a plunging neckline and a short skirt that would be sure to cause a scandal if she wore it out in public. "Although if you stole the body parts of younger women, why do you have to use the cane? And why keep the same deplorable face if you're upgrading the rest of you with beautiful corpses?"

"My, Miss Repute, you certainly are a plucky one, aren't you? Dr. Shelly says that for the first month or so after reanimation, my limbs will be a little stiff and quite frankly, I've gotten used to using the cane. And as for keeping my own head, it was simply good business sense. Dr. Shelly knew unless he was successful, he would not get any more of my money and the good doctor has a great many more experiments he needs funded. The women we used were surplus population, even if they were quite lovely. I took the best of all three, but I was not wild about any of their faces. You, on the other hand, my dear, have lovely bone structure, high cheeks, full lips, and frankly beautiful green eyes. Yours is a face I would enjoy looking at in the mirror each morning."

"Putting aside the psychopathic tendencies needed to kill three women to harvest their body parts, you are aware that Lil is not exactly wealthy. Are you going to be able to adopt and live the poor lifestyle?" Grimstone said.

"I'm far from an idiot, Mr. Grimstone. I met with my lawyer an hour ago to revise my will and I left my estates, fortune, and title to my newly adopted daughter, Lillian Repute. That way, once Dr. Shelly attaches her head to my new body and replaces her brain with mine, I will be able to go on living in my home." Duchess Everlast let her eyes roam up and down the Spellpunk's naked form. "You are a rather handsome man, Mr. Grimstone. I would be happy to allow you to live for the privilege of serving my womanly needs as my consort."

"No thanks. People who murder innocent women aren't on my list of turn-ons."

"Don't talk foolishly. Every man is the same, unable to keep his manhood in his trousers at the sight of a pretty young thing. There is another thunderstorm predicted for tonight and by the morrow, I will be the loveliest creature you have ever seen. If I come to, you will come for me."

"Not at my drunkest," the Spellpunk said.

"Oh no? Watch." The Duchess Everlast ran her young hands up and down Grimstone's chest and down to his legs and then up to stop somewhere in the middle. The patchwork murderess was a bit dismayed by the lack of reaction. She reached in with her other hand and rubbed and pulled. Although there was some change, it was obviously more reflex than excitement.

"But perhaps you wouldn't be concubine material after all. It's clear you must like men."

Lil Repute giggled at the expression on Grimstone's face but was touched to realize she got more of a reaction when Grimstone had simply glanced at her.

Duchess Everlast turned and stared down her nose at Lil. "You find your current predicament amusing?"

"Not particularly. You know this is not going to work. For one thing, I'm a grown woman, so how could you adopt me?"

"It's simply a matter of knowing the right people and paying the right money. It is not an uncommon practice among the aristocracy when one does not have an heir to ensure that the family name lives on."

"What's to stop Shelly from simply attaching my head to

that body and trying to get the money from me?" Lil said.

"For one thing, I'm going to watch him remove your brain before I allow the surgery. It will be a shame to lose that lovely hair, but it would only be temporary until it grows back. Until then, a wig will cover the shaving. I will destroy your brain myself. And even if he decides to put some other brain in, that harlot would not know the passphrase to tell my lawyer in order to validate the will."

"What is the phrase? *Duchess Everlast is a psychotic bitch*?" Grimstone said.

The Duchess looked down her nose at the naked man chained to the table. "Hardly. It's *Duke Everlast had a small manhood*. It's true and unlikely to be spoken by someone else."

The Duchess stepped closer to Lil. "Having a whore in my home is barely acceptable, but having a filthy whore is absolutely not."

The Duchess hung her cane over her forearm and clapped twice. An elderly manservant walked into the room with a bucket and a cloth. He held it up in front of the patchwork murderess. The Duchess reached into the bucket and rung out the rag. She held it over Lil's soot-covered neck and otherwise bare skin.

"Don't touch me."

The Duchess Everlast used the rag to wash off Lil's arm. "Quiet strumpet. What you want matters not. Nor did it ever." Everlast put the rag back in the bucket, repeated the process, then attempted to watch the soot off of Lil's face and was rewarded with a bite to her fingers.

The Duchess let out a small scream and yanked her hand away, staring at the bite marks on her stolen fingers. "How very odd. I reacted mostly by instinct. I barely felt that."

"Sounds like Shelly got sloppy and didn't connect all the nerve endings. That or dying degenerated some of the myelin sheaths. It's quite possible you'll never feel anything quite right again," the Spellpunk said.

"I doubt that, but I'll still be young and beautiful. Regardless of whether or not it hurt, I cannot allow such an attack to go unpunished."

The Duchess slapped Lil across the face. Lil spat at her and she raised her hand in preparation for another slap.

"This is stupid. If you're really going to take my head, why would you want to damage my face and make it less pretty?"

The Duchess nodded a few times. "I never expected such good sense from a strumpet."

The formerly old woman bunched her hands together into a double fist and slammed down on Lil Repute's belly. Lil let loose a muffled scream, trying not to give the Duchess the satisfaction of having hurt her. "I have no need of anything below your neck. Thank you for stopping me from hurting myself. I suggest you enjoy the time you have left. Once the storm begins, I will send Jonathan for you so that Dr. Shelly may take your head for me."

"What about me? Saving me for parts in case you decide you want to become a man?" Grimstone said.

"Don't be droll. You were foolish enough to invade my home, so in punishment, I will simply gift you to Dr. Shelly for his experiments. He expressed excitement over the idea of transplanting tentacles from a squid onto a human frame. You have at least a few days to wallow in your own filth unless you wish to reconsider my concubine offer."

"I'll take my own filth, thank you."

Duchess Everlast swung her cane right at Grimstone's unprotected groin and was rewarded with a high-pitched scream.

The formerly old woman laughed and left

"We better get out of here," Grimstone said a couple of octaves higher than he normally spoke.

"How astute of you to point out something so obvious." There was a booming in the distance and Lil froze. "Was that thunder?"

"I think so. You may not have much time before they come for you. Maybe I can rock this table so it falls over and I can get loose."

Grimstone started rocking his body against the chains. The table shook slightly.

"You do that, Grimstone. I should have known that you can't count on a man to do a woman's job."

Whoever had bound her wrists and ankles to the table had

taken her clothes, weapons, and gadgets, but he hadn't touched her hair. Lil bent her head towards her right hand and managed to free a hairpin she then placed in her mouth. With her fingers, she bent the end and by moving her head and mouth, put the pin in the keyhole. It took some doing and a bit of neck strain, but she was rewarded with a click and the chain fell off.

Lil realized Grimstone was watching and smiling. He started to open his mouth.

"Not one word about my using one of my old skill sets."

"I am ever a gentleman."

"Since when?" With her free hand, Lil used the bent pin to make short work of the other shackles.

"Now free me," the Spellpunk said.

"Quiet! Someone's coming."

Lil picked up the chain that had linked her arms together and put it around her neck like a scarf. She got a good grip around her hairpin and ducked down behind the door. The jigsaw creature was confused by the empty table. Lil took advantage and leaped onto its back, then stabbed the hairpin into one eye, then the other. The gorilla arm threw her across the room, but she managed to take most of the impact on her shoulder. Lil rolled to her feet and put the table between her and the monster. It may have been newly eyeless, but there was nothing wrong with its sense of smell. The jigsaw creature charged right for her. Lil jumped up on the metal table, then jumped over the tiger head, flipping herself so the chain caught on its neck. As she landed, she pulled back. The patchwork creature roared and tried to reach back to tear Lil off, but she held on and pulled the chain tighter. The creature dropped to one knee, then the other. Lil held the chain tight long after the creature stopped moving to make sure it was truly dead.

"Amazing Lil as always."

"Thanks. I've got to go."

"What? You're not going to leave me here like this, are you?" the Spellpunk said.

"I can't risk staying. What if one of them comes back and realizes I'm loose? What if Shelly has another one of these jigsaw creatures?"

"Come on, Lil."

"Don't worry. I'm not leaving you high and dry." Lil pulled her bent hairpin out of the tiger's eye and moved to put it in Grimstone's mouth. "You can use this to pick the locks on your shackles."

"At least wipe it off."

"On what?"

"I don't care."

Lil smiled and wiped the blood and vitreous humor off the pin on the Spellpunk's bare chest.

"You couldn't smear it on the creature's fur?"

"You're whining like a baby. Here's your pacifier."

Lil put the pin between Grimstone's teeth, took the chain, and crept out of the cell. The hallway was empty. Lil silently walked on the balls of her bare feet. When she rounded the first corner, she came face to face with the manservant who had held the bucket for the Duchess. The old man stared for a good ten seconds at the beautiful, nude woman before his servant training kicked in and he brought his head up and stared ahead at eye level.

"Where's your mistress, wrinkles?"

"Down in the laboratory. Shall I escort you there?"

"I don't think so, wrinkles. Take off your shirt and give it to me."

"It would be most unseemly for me to get undressed in front of a woman, let alone a woman of ill repute. It is not what a proper gentleman does."

"Does a proper gentleman allow a woman to go around naked instead of offering her clothes? Or hold a bucket of water while his mistress cleans that same naked woman while she's chained to a table? I suspect a true gentleman would do neither of these things."

"Nor would he remove his clothing. To have a prostitute wearing my shirt would be most unseemly."

"Former prostitute. Why can't people get past that?" Lil rolled her eyes back, then jumped up and down three times. Despite any gentlemen's gentleman training, the old man could not help but stare as bits of Lil bounced beautifully. With his head bent forward, it was a simple matter for Lil to sucker punch the manservant in the jaw with the chain wrapped around her knuckles and knock him out. Bending down to the floor where he landed, she removed his jacket, then his white button shirt and pulled it down over her head. He had small feet for a man, so she also took his shoes and stockings.

As Lil passed a fireplace, she picked up an iron poker. She made her way back to the library where the bookcase door was open, maybe as a courtesy to the jigsaw creature. It would probably have been difficult for it to pull the book out while carrying her unconscious body.

Lil descended the stairs holding the poker in front of her as if it were a rapier. On the last step, her footfall made a sound.

"Jonathan, bring the body over to the table and let me look at it with my own eyes one last time," Duchess Everlast said, as thunder boomed far overhead.

"Jonathan couldn't make it," Lil said.

"Stupid harlot! You'll ruin everything," Everlast said.

"Why are you calling me a harlot? You're the one with syphilis."

"What the blazes are you talking about?"

"Why would you use Bridget's body? The girl had syphilis."

It was a lie, of course, but the Duchess didn't know that

"You assembled my body with a syphilitic harlot!?" Duchess Everlast screamed at Shelly.

"None of the women showed signs of any disease, including syphilis. Even if she was infected, I wouldn't worry about it. She only provided your arms and the same ceptanze in your system that allows the body parts to graft together and stay viable will likely kill the disease.

"You'd better be right, Shelly," she said.

Lil had used the distraction to move in close and smashed the iron poker across the old woman's face in much the same way she had slapped Lil earlier. The jigsaw woman crumbled to the floor.

Dr. Shelly looked from the fallen Duchess back to Lil Repute. "What did you do to my baby?"

"I smacked her across the head. What does it look like?"

"Not her. My Jonathan."

"Let's just say it won't be bothering anyone ever again."

"You barbarous Philistine! Rise up my children and kill this evil woman. Just leave her head intact."

"You really are crazy, Shelly. There's nobody here but you and me."

When the shadows started to move, Lil Repute realized how very wrong she was. The first monstrosity she saw had the head of a fox attached to a human hand as it was shuffling toward her on its fingers. She brought the iron poker down, splitting the monstrosity's skull with the poker.

The next creature that crept from the darkness had the body of a giant tortoise, but the head and neck of a venomous cobra.

Lil swung the poker two-handed. The hooded snake head was torn from the turtle's body to smash into a cabinet. Flying from the shadows on the ceiling came three bats with the heads of kittens trying to bite her. She impaled one and hit the other two hard enough that they crashed to the floor, unable to fly.

Last came the most disturbing of all–the body of a human child with the head and arms of a chimpanzee and the legs of what must've been a grizzly bear cub.

"You sick bastard! Where did you get the child from?"

"His parents sold him to me. The paupers got a very handsome price for him, I might add. He would've died from starvation. At least now his death advanced the cause of science."

The child monstrosity had hesitated and unlike its brothers and sisters, had not attacked.

"Noah, I told you to kill the woman. Obey me."

The jigsaw child reached out and shoved Lil hard enough that she fell to the floor. Instead of pouncing on her, the chimp face whimpered.

Lil got to her knees. "You don't want to hurt me, do you?" The child monstrosity shook his head. "I'm so sorry for what this evil man has done to you."

Lil Repute opened up her arms and pulled the small jigsaw creature in for a hug. It wrapped its chimp arms around her like it was drowning and she was a life preserver, smiling the whole time.

"Don't show it any physical affection. You'll spoil it," Dr. Shelly said. "I knew it was a mistake to use the child's brain instead of the chimp's."

The Duchess regained consciousness and rose to an upright

position. Pulling a sharp blade from the folds of her dress she moved to stab it into Lil's spine.

Noah leaped over Lil and struck Duchess Everlast in the side of the head so hard that she smashed into a wall and crumbled to the floor

Shelly ran to examine her. "She stopped breathing. I only have six minutes to get her brain into a solution of ceptanze or I won't be able to bring her back fully functional," Dr. Shelly said, fumbling for a bone saw.

Lil picked up her poker and pointed it at the mad scientist. "That's not going to happen, Shelly. Put the saw down."

"You don't understand. If she dies, I will not have the money to fund the facilities I need to continue my research. I am able to bridge the gap between living and dead tissue. Think of it. If my research goes as planned, I can make people immortal. If they get old, I will put them in younger bodies. If an organ fails, I can replace it."

"But your twisted immortality comes at a price. You got Everlast's new parts by killing three innocent women."

"Come now, be reasonable. Those women were anything but innocent. In the overall structure of society, they were little more than a boil on its rump, while Duchess Everlast had an enlightened vision and the means to make it a reality. If you allow me to save her brain, I won't take your head for her body. I'll find someone else. What's more, I give you my personal guarantee that when my quest for immortality is complete that I shall share everlasting life with you."

"I don't want to live like that, especially if it costs the lives of others."

"Then you're a fool."

Dr. Shelly lunged and swung his bone saw, but Lil Repute brought up the iron poker and parried it as skillfully as an expert swordsman. Or, as in this case, swordswoman.

Lil brought her knee up into the mad scientist's groin and he curled up into the fetal position on the floor.

"Ow. I can sympathize," the Spellpunk said, leaping out from the bottom of the stairs. He was wearing the manservant's pants, which looked like kickers on the taller man. They couldn't fasten and were held up by suspenders. The jacket likewise was too small to button. "Lil, are you okay?"

"Everlast is dead and Dr. Shelly incapacitated."

The Spellpunk rushed towards Lil, but Noah thought he was attacking, so he leaped up onto the Spellpunk's back and wrapped his hands and clawed paws around Grimstone's torso.

"Another Frankencreature. Don't worry, I'll kill it," Grimstone said.

"No, don't," Lil said. She softened her voice. "Noah, let go of Grimstone. He's a nice man and is not going to harm me, so please don't hurt him, okay?"

The child monstrosity nodded and climbed down off of the Spellpunk's back and moved to cower behind Lil's legs.

"Shelly put the child's brain in it."

The Spellpunk's eyes filled with fury and he kicked Dr. Shelly in the head and his eyes closed. Grimstone was barefoot and ended up hopping and holding his smashed foot.

Once he got himself under control, Grimstone knelt down across from the jigsaw child.

"I'm so sorry about what this man did to you. My name is Jackson Grimstone and I have been looking for my daughter for several years. I will not allow another child to be harmed. I promise you, I will protect you and make sure you have enough ceptanze to survive."

"Why would he need that?" Lil said.

"It's the Bugeye drug that revitalizes tissue and prevents human and animal bodies from rejecting foreign tissue. It's what makes experiments like this possible. I'm sure the Bugeyes gave Shelly some. We'll just have to find it."

The two gawkers were hovering around the Spellpunk as he spoke and he finally noticed. Frowning, he held out his hand. "May I borrow your poker?"

Lil tossed it to him. Grimstone caught it and swung it like a baseball bat and managed to smash the closest gawker into a nearby wall. The other floated back to the opposite side of the lab. He handed the poker back to Lil.

"I guess we better send for the Steam Table Knights."

Noah began tugging on the bottom of Lil's white shirt. She looked down and the jigsaw boy was pointing to where Dr. Shelly had been, *had* being the operative word.

"Looks like the bad doctor has fled. We will just have to wait until he turns up again, I guess," the Spellpunk said.

"How are we going to explain Everlast's corpse? Steam Table Knights frown on somebody killing a member of the aristocracy and will want an investigation, even if the illustrious Spellpunk was involved," Lil said.

Grimstone smiled. "Sometimes, especially if I'm involved. We'll relocate the women's bodies somewhere else where they can be found. I suggest you tell her the butler to take Everlast up to her bed, put her in a full nightgown, then have him notify the authorities that she died in her sleep," Grimstone said.

"Why would he do that?"

"Simple. He'll be obeying the orders of the next Duchess of Everlast. Remember, she did adopt you and named you her official heir and we know the phrase to tell her lawyer."

"Won't the aristocracy have a collective seizure at the idea of me becoming one of them?"

"Heh. I can hope. Some certainly did when I joined. And it wouldn't be the first time someone in your former line of work got a title. A lot of the aristocracy, especially the older ones, have been known to marry their mistresses, many of whom started out being paid for their services."

Lil looked around, then up at the ceiling. "So all this would really be mine?"

"Pretty much. Word on the ballroom circuit is she was worth a pretty penny. Which should be good, because if we're going to keep Noah alive, we'll need money to get ceptanze when Shelly's supply runs out."

"What makes you think I'll be taking care of him?"

"Because that's who you are. You take care of people. You came here to save three women that no one else gave a damn about. You stopped me from hurting the little guy. You won't let anyone else hurt him. And now with your new position and wealth, you'll be able to take care of a lot more people."

"You got a good point there, Grimstone. I'll help you carry the bitch's body upstairs."

"I can handle it myself. And is that any way to talk about your new mommy?"

"Shut up, Grimstone."

The Spellpunk bent down and tossed the old woman's jigsaw

corpse over his shoulder and headed for the stairs.

"Since this will be your new abode, perhaps I can help you break in some of the rooms?"

"Grimstone, is that all you can think about?"

"No, but around you, it's work to keep those thoughts out of my head."

"I'll take the matter under consideration. You're lucky you're cute."

Jackson Grimstone, the Spellpunk

in

Rode Hard

The Spellpunk rolled his eyes and found himself missing his cell phone back on Earth. A call or even a few texts could clarify matters so much more quickly, but instead, all he had was a cryptic letter.

Dear Mr. Grimstone,

The war between the Red Riders and the wolves is spiraling out of control. Too many innocents are dying. Please help us.

The Grand Mere
Order of the Red Hood

The letter left him with far more questions than answers. Still, he was not one to turn down a request for help without good reason, so he put on his top hat and boarded the train to Fableshire.

The Bugeyes who designed Steamworld weren't exactly known for their subtlety. It was loosely designed as a steampunk version of Victorian times, with a few variations thrown in. In addition to the regular theme, there were places like Fableshire that mixed in things like Grimm's fairy tales.

The steam-powered locomotive made good time and its passenger cars were full. One passenger, in particular, grabbed hold of his attention. She was a nubile young woman in a skirt that didn't touch her knees, scandalous for the Victorian society of most of Steamworld. Her top also had a plunging neckline, although that was hardly unusual. But what caught his attention was that the outfit was mostly red and was topped off with a red cloak and matching hood.

Considering her stunning beauty and the amount of flesh

on display, the seats across from her were oddly empty, despite the train being quite crowded.

The Spellpunk strolled over and stopped in front of the woman in red.

"Is this seat taken?"

"I prefer my own company," the woman in red said.

The Spellpunk sat down across from her. "A wise man once sang that you can't always get what you want, but sometimes you might just get what you need. I am paraphrasing, of course."

The woman reached her hand under her cloak and there was no subtlety in the movement. "I think you best go find someplace else to sit. I don't like the company of strangers."

The Spellpunk grinned. "I suppose they don't get much stranger than me, but the situation can be remedied." He took his hat off and with a flourish followed by a mock bow to the woman in red. "My name is Jackson Grimstone. And as easy as that, I am no longer a stranger."

The woman in the red hood merely glared at him unblinking. Grimstone made a show of trying to figure out why she was staring and began touching his shaved head.

"Is my hair all right? One of the drawbacks of wearing hats. Is there something in my hair?"

"You have no hair."

Grimstone let out a sigh. "That's a relief." With a flick of the wrist, he spun his hat. It ended up back atop his head. He leaned forward on his cane, which had a dragon's head for a handle.

"What is one of the famed Red Riders doing so far from home?"

"Not that it's any of your concern, but I had business in Thames."

Grimstone found himself fighting not to roll his eyes at the name of the capital city of the Albion Empire. It had the river London running through it. The Bugeyes were unusually brilliant at world-building, robotics, and genetic engineering, but more than a tad limited in the creativity department, which was more than likely why they created the playworlds.

A small metallic globe with a large lens on one side floated in through an open window in the cabin and took up a position hovering near the pair.

The Spellpunk swung at it with his cane, knocking it two feet back in the air. "Go away. You're not welcome here."

The Red Rider gasped. Almost all the residents of Steamworld had a great reverence for the gawkers and the penalties under law of harming one kept most of the rest from trying.

"You must be either very brave or very foolish," the Rider said.

"Little of both, I'd like to think," Grimstone said.

"Either way, I don't care for your company. I think it best that you leave."

"Unless you bought tickets for this entire train car, I don't see where you have any say in the matter," Grimstone said.

An instant later, the Red Rider pulled her hand from beneath her cloak. A rather large and terribly sharp knife pressed up against Grimstone's Adam's apple. Of course, in that same instant, he pressed the tip of his cane against the nubile young woman's neck.

"I guess we have a Mexican standoff," Grimstone says.

"I have no idea what a Mexican is, but you're a fool to think we're on an even footing. I have a knife forged from the finest steel in the Empire, and you have a walking stick."

"Certainly, one of the Red Riders must realize that not everything is as it seems. Besides, you should know I never bluff."

"I don't even know who you are."

"That's disconcerting. It so rarely happens. Perhaps you know me better from the name the papers gave me. They call me the Spellpunk."

The Red Rider's hand twitched before she steadied it. Grimstone smiled. He had a fearsome reputation and, thanks to the tales in the tabloids, had to make very little of it up himself.

While the two met in their contest of wills, the conductor came by.

"Tickets." He stopped short when he saw the blade and the wooden staff pointed at throats and the gawker floating between them.

The Spellpunk turned his eyes slightly and smiled. "We are a trifle busy right now. Would you mind terribly coming back in a few moments once we've sorted things out?"

The conductor swallowed hard and nodded, then moved on to the next ticket holder.

The Spellpunk turned back to the women in the cloak and hood. "The Red Riders are supposed to work in anonymity. Yet you wear rather striking and recognizable uniforms. How do you think your bosses will react to find out one of their own slit the throat of someone whose death will bring down the wrath of Ireland Yard upon your organization?" Not that Ireland Yard had much love for the Spellpunk, but they did owe him favors several times over. And the Queen found him amusing, so she would likely want the matter investigated.

"Fine. Then we move our weapons…" She used the word with great disdain as she looked at the cane. "… away at the same time."

"No, ladies first. I insist."

The Red Rider took her blade and put it back into the sheath beneath her cloak just as quickly as it came out. Only then did Grimstone move his cane point away.

"Not that I was ever in any real danger."

"Really?" Grimstone said. With the tip of his cane, he opened the top of the basket the woman carried with her. It had goodies, most of them weapons, but still plenty of food. It was in theory supposed to be provided to those who needed it, particularly grandmotherly types. Grimstone held the cane over the basket and pushed the dragon's left eye. A blade popped out, making the woman jump as it speared a red apple.

"You don't mind, I hope. If this food is supposed to be for the needy and the hungry, I fall into at least one of those categories at the moment. Although I have exes who would argue I belong in the other as well."

Grimstone pulled the apple off the blade and took a bite.

"Of course, the real question here is, what would one of

the Red Riders be doing in the city of Thames? Too far for you to ride via your traditional method of steam cycles. Of course, I can only assume it was to either deliver a message or get something too valuable to be trusted to other means of transport."

Grimstone reached over and sorted through the basket. The woman grabbed hold of it and slapped his hand, pulling the basket back.

"Nothing unusual in there and no more than the usual number of hidden compartments."

The Spellpunk reached up upon his hat and pulled goggles down onto his head. He found it amusing that the goggles were such a staple of the steampunk motif, yet he picked them up on another playworld, one with more advanced tech. The goggles did more than just block the wind from his eyes. They had telescopic, microscopic, and a host of other visual settings. One was even able to see through thin objects, which included clothing. First, he looked at the basket, then at the woman. He looked her up, down, then bent over to see her from the inside.

"What are you doing?"

"Checking for danger. You have a very impressive… hidden arsenal. I hadn't even suspected the fourth dagger. A very dangerous place to put it. What happens if you bend over and twist too fast? However, I'm more interested in who wrote the letter and what it says. I can make out the seal, but the writing is difficult, being folded over as many times as it is.

The woman's hand shot up to her right breast. "Also, that mole's not looking too good. Probably should have it checked out."

The woman's hand moved to her left breast.

"You, sir, are a cad and a pig."

"Guess it's better than a pig in a blanket. The wax seal appears to be from lower-level nobility. Are the Riders providing a service or perhaps seeking an alliance?"

"That is none of your business."

"I think it is. Otherwise, I wouldn't have been asked to come and end your war."

"Why would the Red Riders ask the likes of you for the time

of day, let alone assistance?" she said.

Grimstone shrugged. "That's what I'm here to find out. It's not every day I get asked to stop a war."

"The only way to stop the war between the Red Riders and the wolves is to help us slaughter every one of them."

"I'm afraid I'm not into genocide, even of genetically modified human hybrids created by the Bugeyes."

"Are you mad? There is nothing human about the wolves."

"Actually, the first ones started out as human before the Bugeyes got a hold of them. They've had a lot of success stories on this world in terms of their experiments being able to breed, saving them the work of propagating the species."

"I know no Bugeyes, but to suggest a wolf was ever anything resembling human is blasphemous."

"I've been called worse," Grimstone said, as a hooded monk got on to the train and headed towards them. The monk was exceptionally large and well-muscled. "So you're saying the Red Riders should never need help of any kind and could easily spot a wolf anytime or anywhere?"

"Of course, we could. And the only assistance we might require is monetary."

Grimstone raised an eyebrow. "I suppose steam-powered motorcycles don't come cheap. Nor does the fact that none of the Red Riders have gainful employment outside of the order."

"Every Red Rider works every hour of every day to exterminate the wolfen filth."

"I meant something useful."

The Red Rider's hand moved to slap the Spellpunk's face, but he caught it, gently twisted then kissed the top of it. The Red Rider balled her fingers into a fist and punched him on the chin.

"Not bad. If I hadn't had hold of your wrist, it would have hurt."

The large monk in the hooded robe stopped at their seat. His hands were tucked into the sleeves of the opposite arm and his hood covered his entire face in shadow. "Are these seats taken?"

"I'm not sure that would be such a good idea," Grimstone

said as the gawker floated back and forth between all three of them.

"You are really something, speaking such to a man of God. I'm forced to put up with your company, what's one more? Of course, you may join us, brother."

The big man bowed his head. "My thanks, sister."

He stepped between the two and sat on the seat by the window next to the Red Rider. "I am Brother Talbot. What is your name, my child?"

"Gwendolyn."

"And how goes your blessed struggle?"

"As you say, it is a struggle, but we Sisters of the Red Hood fight on."

The large monk nodded. Grimstone rested his hands on his cane, grinning wildly, his head turning back and forth between the two people in hoods.

"What do you find so amusing, Grimstone?" Gwendolyn said.

Grimstone looked at the gawker and winked. "It may make me as bad as the Bugeyes, but this is damn entertaining. Don't mind me. Continue with what you are doing."

"I hear the Sisters of the Red Hood have been having troubles that are financial in nature."

"The Crown has decided that we should be taxed on our lands and properties. Our exemption is no more."

"I had heard as much. I also heard rumors that the sisterhood had turned to the Thames Big Game Society for aid. I cannot help but feel that is a poor decision," said the monk.

"Brother, I do not know how you heard what you have, but I'm forbidden to speak of such things."

"Perhaps I can be of some assistance in these matters," Grimstone said.

"There is absolutely no circumstance under which I would want or need your help," Gwendolyn said.

The monk looked up at the Spellpunk and for an instant, the light from the window showed lupine eyes and a furry face. "I, for one, would welcome it, Sir Grimstone."

"Sir?" the Red Rider said.

Grimstone shrugged. "I rarely use the title. I saved the Queen's life a couple of times. The first time I was knighted. The second I became a peer of the realm, just a baron, though. But I don't much care for titles."

"And I don't care much for your insight."

The large monk sighed. "Sister, is there nothing else you can tell me?"

"No, I'm sorry."

"So am I."

The monk bent forward, his face pressed up against Gwendolyn's chest and torso as he made a sniffing sound.

"Brother, my order's not sworn to celibacy, but yours is. This is most unseemly."

"Then I must apologize again."

The monk took his hand out of his sleeve. There were claws at the end of it. He reached out for the right side of her chest and tore the material away. The sealed letter was between his fingers. "And I apologize for the third and last time."

The monk climbed out the open window, which seemed too small to accommodate someone of his bulk.

Gwendolyn looked down at her exposed undergarment, her eyes wide and her mouth open.

"That man tore my clothes. What sort of gentleman are you to just sit there and watch instead of lending me aid?"

"I never claimed to be a gentleman. In fact, I seem to recall you telling me that you would never, under any circumstances, require my help. I took you at your word. Although I would think you would be more concerned about what's missing than what's showing.

The Red Rider climbed out the window towards the top of the train. The Spellpunk took off his hat and put it on the rack above the seats, then leaned his own head out the window and looked up. Pulling back into the cabin, he put the tip of his finger in his mouth and stuck it out the window as the gawker watched.

"I think not." The gawker out the window flew to the top of the train as Grimstone choose to stroll to the space between the train cars and use the ladder there to climb up to the top of the train. Grimstone went into a low crouch and carefully moved towards the Red Rider and the wolf in monk's clothing. Gwendolyn had a knife out. A flintlock pistol lay on the top of the train. The Spellpunk assumed it was the first weapon the hooded woman had tried before it was knocked aside by the wolf.

"Give me back the letter," she demanded.

"I can't do that. If this letter contains what I think it does, it could spell extinction for my people."

"Exactly," Gwendolyn said, swinging her knife at the wolf, who leaned over backward while grabbing hold of the hilt and plucking it away. The woman went down to all fours, then kicked out to his knee with her boot, followed up with a rapid second kick to his groin. The wolf was still male and doubled over. Gwendolyn spun and brought her elbow into his face. The wolf stood as if nothing had happened.

The Red Rider charged at him just as the train was turning. The wolf spun and the woman went over and off the side of the train. The wolf in monk's clothes grabbed hold of the Red Rider's cape and pulled her back from a certain fall and potential death. When she got to the roof, another knife was in her hand. The wolf quickly took the blade and tossed it over the side.

The train lurched again and the Rider kicked hard against the same knee she kicked earlier. Talbot fell over backward and would have tumbled off the train if the Spellpunk hadn't reached out with his cane and pulled the wolf back into an upright position on top of the train.

"You saved the foul beast!?" Gwendolyn said.

"No, I saved a person who is a trifle furry."

"This will not be over until one of us lies dead," Gwendolyn said.

Talbot was not nearly as bloodthirsty as the hooded woman and didn't say a word.

"I think it's time you left quickly," the Spellpunk said.

"I can stop the woman from hurting me or herself," Talbot said.

"But she won't be alone for long." Grimstone pointed to the

horizon where three Red Riders were approaching the train on steam-powered motorcycles. They had much larger weapons.

"I see your point. Good day, Sir Grimstone. We shall meet again."

"I look forward to it."

The gawker had been hovering off the side of the train to capture the fight and followed the wolf as he leapt off the opposite side of the train and landed on the ground rolling. The impact would have knocked the wind out of a regular man, even breaking some bones or snapping a spine, but Talbot simply stood and started running. The wolf was faster than a regular human, but far slower than steam bikes. However, the hills weren't far and he made it to cover while the trio of Red Riders were still in the distance. The gawker came back to hover between Grimstone and Gwendolyn.

"You let him get away!" Gwendolyn said.

"I don't think he was your enemy," Grimstone said as he climbed down.

"He's a wolf Of course, he's my enemy." The Rider followed him down the ladder. "All they want is the death of good people, especially the Sisters of the Red Hood!"

"I think you're wrong on that count too. Talbot had his claws against your chest and could've just as easily ripped your heart out as torn your bodice. He took the letter, yet didn't even scratch your skin. Then on top of the train, he had two of your knives and didn't even try to use either on you. If wolves are so evil, why didn't he even try to harm you? Why save your life?"

"Wolves are the enemy of humanity. They attack children lost in the woods and old women in their homes."

"And blow down straw and wood houses."

The Red Rider stared at Grimstone. "What in the Red Hood are you talking about?"

Grimstone sighed and pressed on. "Have you ever stopped to think that maybe that was all just propaganda?"

"I've seen what the wolves have done."

"Yet I'm sure you've done far worse to them. I've never heard of a wolf hanging human heads on the wall, but can the same be said of the Red Riders?"

Gwendolyn shut up and waved at her sisters. They went back inside the car until the train reached the station.

Gwendolyn got off before the train even stopped. The Spellpunk put his hat back on and fell in behind her.

"Where do you think you're going?"

"My presence has been requested at the Covent of the Red Hood. You may take me to see the Grand Mere."

Gwendolen walked faster, but Grimstone simply followed. The Spellpunk stopped and watched as the trio of Red Riders got off their steam cycles. It was hard not to stare, but at least he didn't have his drooling face pressed to the train window like some of the other passengers. Gwendolen's outfit was quite conservative compared to the miniskirts and plunging necklines of the other three. For whatever reason, the nonhuman Bugeyes seemed to really enjoy their cheesecake, at least the human variety. Even on a playworld that was set in a time when women were considered second-class citizens, women rose up to prove the Bugeyes wrong. Grimstone didn't necessarily agree with the wholesale slaughters committed by the Red Riders, but at least they believed they were trying to make their world a better place.

"Welcome back, Sister Gwendolyn," said one of the new women in a cloak and hood, blonde hair peeking out from underneath. "Who is this? Have they sent a representative to negotiate?"

"No, this is an annoyance who claims to be the Spellpunk. He is simply following me."

As one, the three women reached beneath their red cloaks.

Grimstone smiled and put his hands up at his side. Thanks to his goggles, he could see that they were all reaching for flintlocks.

"Ladies, there is no need for violence here. I've been summoned to help your situation, so please take me to the Grand Mere and we will sort everything."

"I was unaware of the Grand Mere asking for help. Why wouldn't she have told me?" said the blonde Rider.

Grimstone put his arms down as the women had removed their hands from their cloaks and shrugged. "I can't rightly say.

Does she tell you everything?"

"Nearly. I am her second-in-command."

"Excellent, then I'll ride with you."

"We're not going back yet. A wolf disguised himself as a brother and attacked me, then stole the letter," Gwendolen said, pulling her cloak aside and revealing her torn bodice. "He fled towards the hills on the other side of the train."

"Are you hurt?" the blonde said.

"Not to worry, Melinda. I'm unharmed."

"You're lucky you survived him getting that close," Melinda said.

"I pointed that out too. Perhaps this wolf is not your enemy," Grimstone said.

Melinda looked at him as if he were an idiot child. "You obviously do not know much about wolves. Are you aware that they live solely to maim, kill, and destroy?"

"People can change."

"Wolves are not people."

"This wolf could've killed Gwendolyn at least twice, yet he didn't even scratch her. Makes you wonder if wolves are so bloodthirsty, why would he not harm her? And if one wolf is different, then perhaps more are."

"We will search the hills until we will find the beast," Melinda said.

"Good luck with that then. I'll wait here for you to pick me up so we can go speak with the Grand Mere." Grimstone sat in a wooden chair on the platform, leaning it back against the station wall and putting his feet up on a support beam. "Happy hunting."

The woman hopped on their cycles and rode into the hills. A few hours later, they returned empty-handed.

"No luck?" Grimstone said.

"I don't want to speak of it. Get on the back," Melinda said.

"Love to." Grimstone climbed on the back of the bike, then looked at his hands and back at the Red Rider. "I don't want to act inappropriately, but I was wondering where would be a proper place for me to hold on to?"

"Hold on to the seat behind you. Should your grubby little

paws so much as touch me, I will toss you from the bike and grind you into dust with my wheels."

"That's okay, but you really should buy me dinner and drinks before asking me to get that physical with you. Although I've got to wonder why such little protective gear? Where I come from, cycle riders tend to wear leather in case of spills and helmets to protect their heads."

"I guess the people where you come from are not very good riders."

"Some are, some aren't. That's the problem with generalizations. They can be right and wrong at the same time. And doesn't it get cold riding with your outfit being so open the front like that? From my limited experiences with cycle riding, it seems like most people worry about bugs flying into their mouths. It must be terrible having to worry about them crashing into your cleavage."

Melinda tried hard not to chuckle. "We simply save them as snacks for later on."

Grimstone and the Sisters of the Red Hood rode off into the sunset.

As they approached the mansion-sized convent that served as the Red Riders' headquarters, the Spellpunk let out a sigh of relief. When the bike came to a halt, Grimstone climbed off and stretched his arms up over his head.

"Smooth ride?" Melinda said.

"For around here, it ain't bad, but you really could work on building up the shocks. A large metal coil will do the trick."

The Red Rider thought about it and nodded her head. "That might work at that. I'm going to go speak to the Grand Mere and find out what's going on."

Melinda and Gwendolyn walked up the stone staircase that led to the front of the convent where a woman in her late fifties walked out to meet them and the gawker reappeared. The Grand Mere's hood and cape were much more elaborate, but she wore the same style of red outfit, only not showing as much leg. The three women exchanged words and the Grand Mere frowned. She walked to the top of the staircase and looked down at Grimstone.

"So you are truly the one the press calls the Spellpunk?"

"In the flesh," Grimstone said with a smile.

"I'm not impressed. I also did not summon you." By this point, over two dozen women had made their way outside and up onto the roof, which was designed with a walkway and cover to hide behind in case of attack.

"Now wait just one second." Grimstone set one foot on the stairs and twenty-five women pointed either a crossbow or a flintlock gun or rifle at him. Grimstone put his hands above his head and stepped back down slowly. "I have your letter in my pocket."

As he moved to put his hand in the pocket, the group of women lifted their weapons higher. "Any of you ladies are welcome to get it out for yourselves."

The Grand Mere nodded to Melinda, who strutted down the stairs.

Grimstone gently pulled open his jacket and the woman reached inside his breast pocket.

"Don't let me catch you trying to cop a feel."

"Not even in your dreams," Melinda said, taking the letter out. She returned up the stairs and handed the paper to the Grand Mere, who opened and read it.

"This is not from me, although it does look like our stationary and the postmark shows that it originated in Fableshire," the Grand Mere said.

"Perhaps one of your Red Riders sent it?"

"Nonsense. None of my girls would do something like this without my permission.

"Why would you want peace?" the Grand Mere asked. "I don't see why you would object to us inviting the Thames Big Game Society here to help eradicate the wolves once and for all. Wasn't one of your well-publicized exploits an adventure with the Society? Something involving dinosaurs, if I remember correctly," the Grand Mere said.

"It's true. I've helped them on an occasion or three, but the truth of the matter is I'm not one who hunts for sport. Something more has to be involved–hunger, curiosity, even vengeance. And one of the key differences between some of the members of the Big Game Society and myself is that I do not hang the heads of sentient beings on my wall as trophies."

The Grand Mere's face darkened and her eyes narrowed into slits. "Calling the wolves sentient is almost as bad as calling them human."

"They once were human before the Bugeyes' genetic engineers got a hold of them. Wolves are one of their more stable experiments, so they are able to reproduce on their own."

"You keep referring to the mythical masters of this world, which all rational beings know is nothing but nonsense and poppycock."

Grimstone looked at the gawker floating nearby. "You hear that? The lot of you are nonsense and poppycock, so please kindly leave us alone since you don't exist."

The gawker and Grand Mere ignored him. "The wolves made a bargain with a demon and were transformed into the creatures they are today because of it. They live only to destroy lives, both those they kill and those they don't. They have a special fondness for little girls and adult women."

"The Bugeyes are nasty creatures, doing whatever they can for programming and content. They wanted to create something based on a fairytale from my world. I've heard how a wolf attacked you and killed your grandmother."

"It didn't just kill her, it devoured her. And a kind woodsman who came to our aid. It would've eaten me as well, except it didn't expect a child to be able to swing an axe hard enough to cleave his head in two. Ever since that day, I have devoted my life to ridding the world of these vermin. I fought the good fight for decades, but now my family inheritance is nearly gone. If I don't secure funding, I'll have to put these girls out on the street to survive on their own."

"The Bugeyes are not above drugging or programming people to behave how they want them to. The wolves may not be what you think they are. You can negotiate peace to end the violence. That way, everyone wins," Grimstone said.

"Negotiate a peace with beasts? It wouldn't even be worth the paper it was written on. They have no concept of honor or kindness. They would break the treaty the first opportunity that presented itself," the Grand Mere said.

"Is there anything that can be done to change your mind?" Grimstone said.

"The only way to peace is the extermination of their species."

"For there to be a peace treaty, both sides have to be interested, so I guess it would be foolish for me to continue to try," Spellpunk said, noticing the slight widening of Melinda's pupils. "I came all this way for a wasted trip."

"Your trip may not have been in vain, Grimstone. The beast still has the letter from the Thames Big Game Society, which I hope is an offer from them to finance the Red Riders in exchange for our opening our borders for them to hunt the wolves. There should even be a large check sealing the deal. We need that money. Help us get the letter and the check back from the wolf, and I will grant you one favor from any or all of the Red Riders."

"Any favor I ask? Even from you, Grand Mere?"

The old woman nodded. "Even myself. Think about it. My girls are well trained and are, in fact, a small army. I've heard enough of your exploits to know that there will come a time when you might need our help."

"Sure enough. How about we make it two favors, one for the letter and one for the check?" Grimstone said.

The Grand Mere frowned. The Spellpunk smiled.

"Very well. Two favors. My word on it."

"And I guess you best give me a crash course in wolf hunting."

"I will leave that distasteful task to Melinda," the Grand Mere said.

Gwendolyn laughed. "Better you than me, Sister."

The Spellpunk stuck his tongue out at the one Rider and smiled and waved at the other. Melinda rolled her eyes and seemed none too thrilled by the prospect.

The blonde woman took him to their weapons training area. "Before I allow you to participate in an actual wolf hunt, you need to prove that you're proficient and will not be slain in the attempt."

"Lady, I'm the Spellpunk. I tend to survive whatever is

thrown at me."

"That's all fine and good for the city, but you're in Red Rider country. You can't count on the coppers to save you." Grimstone chuckled. "You think this is funny? Your life and the lives of those with you may depend on what you learn here."

"If you say so. Show me what you've got and let's get this over with."

The Red Rider loaded an arrow into a crossbow and aimed at a target twenty-five feet away. Melinda pulled the trigger and the bolt pierced the center of the bullseye.

"When you can match that you can laugh at my training."

"Promise?" Grimstone said, taking the crossbow and loading it. He used his goggles to gauge the distance as well as other factors like wind and the line of the fletching, then lifted it straight up at his side.

"No, you're doing it wrong. That's not how you hold it..."

Grimstone put his finger over his lips. "Shush."

Grimstone turned his head away from the target to wink at the Red Rider. Without turning his head back, the Spellpunk pulled the trigger and the bolt split Melinda's in half.

Grimstone was still looking at the Red Rider when her eyes went wide and her mouth opened.

"Did I hit it?" Grimstone said, then turned to see his handiwork. "Oh, goody, this means I can laugh now. Ha, ha."

"Beginner's luck."

"You know damn well no beginner ever made a shot like that, so let's get to the rest of what you consider training so you can teach me what I actually need to know, including why you sent me that letter."

"I... sent you no letter."

"Yes, you did. You even hesitated a moment, just now, before denying it. I know it was you, but I just don't know why yet. Care to enlighten me?"

"I can't enlighten you about something that never happened."

"I get that a lot. I can wait and, who knows, I might learn something."

By the end of the day, the Spellpunk had proved himself

proficient and finished his Red Rider training. Nothing as spectacular as his opening salvo, but he was at least proficient in all areas. Refusing to give him his own red cloak, Melinda instead brought him to the Order's library.

Despite the existence of printing press technology, many folks on Steamworld still had scribes write up books by hand. Hand-printed books were much more expensive, but people like the Order preferred to keep their knowledge, while not secret, at least available only to select sources.

The Spellpunk selected several tomes and sat down at a table. Melinda stood over him.

"I'll likely be here all night. You can toddle off to bed and get some rest," Grimstone said.

"And leave the likes of you alone with our sacred writings? Never."

The Spellpunk shrugged. "Suit yourself."

The Order of the Red Hood's forty-plus year history had been a bloody one, with over two hundred recorded kills. Not all of them had been wolves, although most had. The Order hunted other so-called monsters as well. They had a relatively low casualty count, which Grimstone pointed out to his watcher.

"That's because of the training the Red Riders have," Melinda said.

"I think it's more due to the fact that the wolves really don't have any decent weapons and are forced to live in the wild, due to some nonsensical Fableshire law that prevents them from owning property and punishes anyone caught aiding them or giving them a place to live. Sort of easy to shoot unarmed fish in a barrel with a crossbow or gun."

"Finish your work, so can both get some rest," Melinda said. Grimstone raised an eyebrow, noting that the Red Rider didn't dispute his claim.

Melinda endeavored to stay awake, but eventually fell asleep in her chair, her red cloak beside her on the table. Grimstone finished and gently picked up her cloak and draped it around her. He left her to sleep and returned to his quarters.

Barely two hours later, Grimstone woke abruptly when

his cot was lifted up, and he was tossed to the floor. He came rolling up in a crouch, the tip of his cane pointed toward the invader in his room.

"That was a very rude awakening. Have you ever heard of knocking before throwing someone out of their bed? Or even bringing them breakfast."

"How dare you sneak off!" Melinda's face was almost as red as her cloak.

"I didn't sneak off. I went to bed. It's not my fault that you are a lightweight and couldn't stay awake," Grimstone said.

"How dare you!? Get up so we can head out to try to accomplish our mission."

"Sure. A question before we go–is breakfast in bed totally out of the question?"

His answer was a slammed door.

Melinda spent the better part of the day riding Grimstone around the countryside, looking at abandoned shacks in the woods, caves, and even a treehouse, none of which had seen an occupant in quite some time. Most were covered with cobwebs.

"I've had enough of the runaround. The question is why are you giving it to me?"

"This is how a proper hunt is conducted," the Red Rider said.

"You're about as full of crap as the Thames sewer system. That or I think the two hundred kills in your record book are greatly exaggerated. You're trying to keep me from finding this wolf. The question is why? Do you want the glory of finding him for yourself? Or is it something else?"

Grimstone had been riding a sidecar on the steam cycle and suddenly found himself thrown up into the air and landed hard on his seat.

"Stop and let me out," Grimstone said.

"You're getting out because I hit a bump? It's not as if I did it on purpose," Melinda said.

"I saw you swerve to make sure I hit it, but that's not why I told you to stop. The Brotherhood of the Whispering Moon has a monastery here and I'm going to go investigate it."

"There are no signs. How could you possibly know that?"

Grimstone lifted his wrist. "My watch is a compass, and I memorized the map of this area before coming here."

"You memorized the map?"

"It took me about an hour and a half. I don't have a photographic memory, but I was a teacher and do all right for myself."

"Why would you think the wolf is there? Because he stole one of their robes before boarding the train to attack Gwendolyn and you?"

"I don't think Talbot stole the robe. I think it was gifted to him. And if you were seriously looking for Talbot, that would've been the first place you took me to."

"I'm not going to waste my time on a wild goose chase."

Grimstone twirled his cane and started walking up the dirt road. "Fine by me, although where else are you going to go?"

"I'm leaving. You'll end up having to walk back to the convent," Melinda said.

"I've traveled between worlds. On foot. I don't think five miles on a dirt road is going to do me any harm."

"You're wasting your time!"

Grimstone waved without looking behind him. "So you say. Good day."

A half-hour later he arrived at the monastery of the Order of the Whispering Moon. As he approached, the gawker that had followed him was caught and trapped in a metal net. Although it tried, it was unable to free itself.

The Spellpunk knocked on the massive doors. The place was built like a fortress, with stone walls fifteen feet high.

A small slot about eye level slid open and a pair of eyes stared out of him.

"We do not welcome visitors here. Go in peace."

Grimstone adjusted his goggles and looked through the door at the monk behind it, then took his hat off and bowed his head slightly. "Be that as it may, your order has welcomed me before. My name is Jackson Grimstone and I seek the truth. I believe you have a wolfman here to whom I wish to speak."

"We would never harbor such a creature," the monk said.

"Nonsense. We both know your order is quite aware of the

fact that we live on a playworld known as Steamworld and that you work tirelessly to thwart the Bugeyes. A cause, I might add, I myself find quite worthy. Like myself, many of you are from Earth and were transported here against your will. I've no intention of harming Talbot, I merely wish to speak to him. Besides, what do you have to worry about? You've got two snipers in either tower with Earth-style rifles focused on me right now."

Grimstone could tell the monk was smiling just from the change in appearance of his eyes. "We've heard of you, Mr. Spellpunk. You stick it to the Bugeyes quite well, even if you allow gawker cameras to follow you around. Those are never allowed inside."

"A sensible policy. Nice trap, by the way. How long will it hold the gawker?"

"Long enough for you to complete your visit and be on your way. That is assuming that the person in question wishes to speak with you."

"Fair enough."

The gawker was flying back and forth so the net rubbed and bent the wires against the tree and made a small enough hole to squeeze out through.

"That's a first," the monk said, hustling the Spellpunk through the door. The monk managed to slam the door shut an instant before the gawker made it to the door jamb.

"It's going to be looking for a way in," Grimstone said.

"Let it," said the monk. "All the walls are stone and all the doors are three-inch thick wood. It is a pleasure to meet you, Jackson. Call me Brother Tim, but my full name is Timothy Shannon. Born and raised in Woodside, New York in the good old USA until the Bugeyes got a hold of me."

"I was going to guess New York by your... ahem religious symbol. I take you're a Yankees fan," Grimstone said.

"All the way. What about you?

"Red Sox."

"Funny, you don't look like the devil. Maybe you have better taste in football. I've made Jets and Giants medals as well."

"Buffalo Bills."

"Wow, you really do root for the underdog."

"Speaking of the underdog…"

Brother Tim nodded. "My backup on the door has already gone to fetch Talbot."

"Good." Grimstone reached into his pocket and pulled out a small leather billfold. "Before we go see him, I have a question on a personal matter. The Bugeyes separated me from my daughter. I ended up on another playworld, but found that she was somewhere on Steamworld, so I made my way here. I've yet to find her. This is a picture of her when she was six. She should be nine now. Have you with any of the monks heard about a girl from Earth, thinking she was an orphan?"

Brother Tim took the picture and looked at it. "I'm sorry, Jackson, but I haven't. With your permission, I'd like to make a copy of this and circulate it among the brothers just in case."

"You have that level of technology?"

Brother Tim smiled. "In a sense. Come with me, I'll show you."

The monk led the Spellpunk on a few twists and turns through corridors that ended up in a room with several desks. On the walls were drawings and paintings of major cities on Earth, as well as other memories of home. A half-dozen men sat at tables with paper and charcoal drawing over pictures that were illuminated. A seventh placed papers beneath a light that projected the image six times for the men to copy.

"You made a light box," Grimstone said.

"With a few modifications. We get six images to copy instead of one through a series of mirrors and lights. It is not exactly mass production, but for steam age technology, it's what we have and gives a better quality picture than a woodcutting in less time. With your permission, I will make copies of the picture."

"Can you just photograph it?"

"We will do that as well, but it will be black-and-white while our artists will be able to add some color."

"Thank you."

Brother Tim gingerly placed the photograph on the larger table and made some adjustments, so the image was enlarged as it was lit on six pieces of paper. The monk artists got to work as did the man who had been placing the papers.

"He doesn't use the lightbox?" Grimstone said.

"Brother Michael has exceptional skills. Watch."

The man's hands moved with speed and grace. Before the others were even halfway tracing he finished and held it up. Grimstone looked from the drawing back to the picture. They were not the same image.

Brother Michael smiled. "Back in the real world, I was a police sketch artist. You said she should be about nine, so I extrapolated what she would look like now. Back home, I had computer programs to do this, but I found I was more accurate than the programs."

Grimstone tenderly took the drawing and looked like he might cry. "May I keep this?"

"Of course. I'll make another and then put that on the lightbox for the others to copy as well. You never know, it might help find her."

"If it does, I'll be forever in your debt."

"I am honored to help."

"Thank you."

Grimstone was led into another room where the wolf was waiting. Talbot still wore the robe, but his hood was down, revealing a fur-covered head and ears. There were higher than a normal man and looked far more canine.

The wolf extended his hand and the Spellpunk shook it.

"Thank you for saving me from falling back on the train."

"You're welcome, Talbot."

The wolf bowed his head. "That is the name I tell others. My given name is Fido."

The Spellpunk's eyebrows raised, and he looked at Brother Tim.

"I know. I've even explained it to him," said the monk.

"You're coming from the Order of the Red Hood? Do you have any message for me?"

Everything clicked into place for the Spellpunk. "No, Melinda never even mentioned she knew you. In fact, she is trying to track you down right now and she led me on a bit of a wild goose chase. So how long have the two of you been a couple?"

"Since she tried to kill me and accidentally set the tavern we were in on fire. Several human patrons succumbed to the smoke. I stopped fighting with her long enough to get them out. She followed me into the night woods after that and fell off a cliff in the dark. I nursed her back to health and in the process, we fell in love."

"Not deep enough for her to leave the order apparently," Grimstone said.

"It's not that simple. The order has killed people for leaving and if it ever came out that she had carnal relations with one of the enemies of the order, none of them would rest until we were both found, tortured, and painfully killed."

"Can't argue with that assessment. Couldn't you simply just run off together somewhere else?"

"Where else would have us?"

"There are parts of Albion that are surprisingly liberal and have all sorts of races living together. Same with Hoodoo. You might even get by in parts of Thames. Although many mixed marriages are frowned upon there, it stops short of actual criminal prosecution. Plus, in the city, if the Order came after you, the Steam Table Knights and police would protect you," Grimstone said.

"That's not my only responsibility." The large wolf motioned for Grimstone to follow him into the next room where three Wolf children were playing with a ball.

"Yours?"

"Their parents were killed by the Order, I was left to raise them."

A red ball bounced and landed by the Spellpunk's feet. He knelt to pick it up. One of the wolf children, a girl, ran over and he handed her the ball. "How old are you?"

"Nine," the little girl answered, then ran back to play with the other two.

Brother Tim walked and stood beside the Spellpunk who was staring after the fur-covered girl. "These children were born this way, not mutated. She could not be your daughter."

The Spellpunk nodded and wiped his eye. "So Fido, you're the reason Melinda wrote the letter to me."

The wolf nodded. "You have quite the reputation for being able to turn manure into miracles. We had nowhere else to turn and nothing to lose."

"That explains how you knew about the Thames Big Game Society sending the check. Do you still have them both?" Grimstone asked.

The wolf nodded.

"If you're willing to give them to me, I may have a way to get you and Melinda out of this safely, but unfortunately, stopping the war by having a peace treaty is simply not possible. The Red Riders would not honor it for long. I may be able to arrange for you all to move to an area where the Red Riders would not be able to come after any of you. Would that be acceptable?"

"You include the children in that?"

"Of course.

"Then I would, though I can't speak for Melinda."

"I'll ask her myself."

"Will you see her tonight?"

The Spellpunk shook his head. "No. It's late and the monks have offered me a place to stay for the evening. I'll talk to her about it in the morning. I'm sure she's camped out watching this place."

As the sun rose, so did the monks. The Spellpunk took a little longer. After breakfast, he exited the monastery to find the gawker floating and waiting. He tipped his hat to it, then gave it the finger.

Grimstone walked down the path and within moments of reaching the main road heard the rumbling of the steam cycle and turned to see Melinda riding towards him.

"Good morning. I trust you slept well," Grimstone said.

The Red Rider simply glared.

"Not a morning person, I take it."

"Grimstone you are the most arrogant, inconsiderate, slimy man I've ever had the displeasure of meeting. I've got a good mind to leave here and let you walk back," she said.

"But then you won't find out the wonderful solution I

worked out for you and your lover. Not to mention see me deliver the letter and the check to the Grand Mere." Grimstone held up a cloth sack. "And most unfortunate of all, you'll miss out on this breakfast that Fido made for you."

"So you know."

Grimstone nodded. "Although to be truthful, I already had my suspicions. Now I have confirmation."

"Are Fido and the children all right?"

"They're all fine. The monks are taking good care of them."

"So you figured a way to broker peace?"

"Heavens, no. But I have figured out a way for the five of you to have a chance."

"How?"

"It's best that you don't know yet. Now eat your breakfast, so we can get going."

Grimstone handed her the cloth sack and she sat on the ground and opened it. She looked at the food, then lifted something that looked partially eaten and held it out towards the Spellpunk. "What's this?"

"I had part of the sausage. Who knew when you were going to pick me up and it was a long walk down to the main road and I got hungry."

Sometime later, the pair were back in front of the Grand Mere.

"You have the letter and the check already?" the Grand Mere asked.

"Of course. Was there ever any doubt?" Grimstone said.

"How did you find the beast?" the Grand Mere said to Melinda who looked to be turning a sickly shade of green. "He was a crafty one."

"We split up to cover more ground. I was alone when I found him," Grimstone said.

"For you to have the letters, you must've killed him, correct?" the Grand Mere said.

"I daresay he'll trouble you no more," Grimstone said.

"Excellent. Give them to me."

"Not so fast. There is still the matter of my two favors."

"Grimstone, you may have a fearsome reputation, but

there's no way you could stop my girls from simply killing you and taking the check and letter from your corpse," the Grand Mere said.

The Spellpunk held up the documents between his hands. "I'll give you that, but you couldn't get to me before I ripped them both in half, which would render them useless."

Guns were raised. "The lasses are quite swift."

"Your reputation and honor would suffer."

The Grand Mere had a dry smile. "It would recover."

"We had a deal."

"Deals are made to be broken."

"So they are, which is why I took a few precautions before I met back up with Melinda. In fact, I documented our dealings in great detail and sent a letter out in the post to a reporter friend at The Thames Gazette. I sent out a second letter with a photograph of both check and letter to another friend. If I am killed or do not return home by tomorrow, she has instructions to bring the photo to the reporter, which will undoubtedly run on the front page along with the news of my death. I wonder what outrage that story will cause. Particularly to the members of the Thames Big Game Society who state in this very letter about the need for utter secrecy. I believe there is explicit mention that the deal will be broken should the details contained within ever be revealed. Which, of course, was why you had to send the lovely Sister Gwendolyn to fetch it for you all the way from Thames rather than risk the post yourselves. Not only will you have torn documents, but the entire financial arrangement you worked so hard to broker will be null and void. You and the ladies will be out on the streets. A pity. So kill me or honor our deal and grant me my favors. Your call."

"Very well, I will grant your favors. What are they?"

"I've been very impressed with your organization. So impressed that I would very much appreciate it if the Order of the Red Hood and any of its members or associates did not operate in Thames. In fact, I insist that if any of you even want to visit the city, you must have my permission first."

"That's outrageous! What if we were called to visit Her Majesty? Would I tell Queen Theodora that I had to refuse because Jackson Grimstone didn't want me to come?" the Grand Mere said.

"Teddie invites you to tea often, does she?" Grimstone said. For a moment. The Grand Mere lost her regal bearing and became flustered. Grimstone nodded. "I've been a few times myself. The finger sandwiches are amazing, aren't they?"

"It has not happened yet, but in my heart, I know she approves of the work we do here and one day will either reward or thank us for it."

"Very well. I shall agree to make an exception if the Queen ever does send you her personal invitation. However, barring that, the Red Riders will stay out of my city. Those are the terms of my first favor. The second one, I will name at a later date. I have all the details written down here." Grimstone unrolled three identical large pieces of paper with everything written on them, including naming the second favor later. The Spellpunk added in the bit about the Queen. "I would like you as well as all the Red Riders to sign them. That way there is no confusion with anyone."

"Very well, but who is the third copy for?"

"Teddie."

"You will give our agreement to the Queen?"

"Of course. How else will she know of our provision involving her?" Grimstone had originally intended to give it to a friend as added insurance, but his new idea assured the Order would never overtly break the agreement knowing that the Queen was aware.

The Grand Mere and all the Red Riders present signed the document. The Riders got one, Grimstone the other two.

"We've done as you asked. Now give me the letter and the check."

With a bow and a flourish, Grimstone presented both. "Now if you don't mind, I'd like to catch the next thing smoking back to Thames."

"And to make certain that you do, Melinda will accompany you to the station and ensure sure you get on the train."

"Very well. It's easier than walking."

Neither Melinda nor Grimstone said a word until they were

miles away from the convent. "That was your plan? To keep the Red Riders out of your city?"

"Of course. Now all you have to do is hop on the train with me, probably bring your little bike, and your sisterhood can't touch you. Or Fido and the kids. I've invited them to live with me until Fido gets on his feet and finds a job. You're welcome to come visit. Supervised of course."

"But what will I do for work?"

"You're a very capable woman, and there are many women who would prefer a female bodyguard over a male."

"What about Fido…"

"He and the cubs and a bunch of other wolves should already be on the train in a few large, but comfortable packing crates. That way there are no worries about them being seen by a spy working for the Order of the Red Hood or someone with a big mouth. I'm sure many more will follow before the hunters from the Thames Big Game Society arrive."

"Grimstone, I don't know what to say. Thank you."

"Nonsense, it's what I do. And you will sign a document as well, stating that you owe me a favor at some point in the future too."

The soon-to-be former Red Rider nodded. When she boarded the train, she did so with a smile.

Colonel Windglass and the Skyrovers
in

TOUCHING THE SKY

Reginald Windglass woke drunk and screaming, visions of the past torturing him right on schedule. He hated that the only way he seemed able to remember his wife and children was as bloody and butchered.

Reginald lifted his head off the smooth bar and was greeted with a vision of his reflection in a mirror looking back. He turned his head left and right as he stared at his reflection and ran his fingers through his gray hair.

"I'm too young to be this damn old."

"Don't worry, Gramps, me, and my boys will entertain you in your old age. Unless you are willing to pay to not see the show," said a man who thought he was tough as long as he was surrounded by five other men who supposed they were just as tough.

"Buy me and my pals a round and we'll leave you to wallow in your misery."

A short barrel of a man walked over to stand beside Windglass. "Colonel, are these ruffians bothering you?"

"Nothing I can't handle, Sergeant Hornblower."

"Colonel? Imitating an officer in the military is a crime, Gramps. I'm not sure Her Majesty would approve.

"I assure you Queen Theodora approves of everything Reginald Windglass does," Jacob Hornblower said.

The gang of toughs laughed. "Are you trying to tell us that this pathetic, fat, bloated imitation of a man is the hero of the Hoodoo Wars? The man who brought a century of conflict to an end with what is arguably the finest peace treaty ever signed?" the leader of the toughs said.

"They're full of crap. Windglass was a general, not a colonel," said another.

"I was, but I was a better man when I was a colonel. Happier too. So that is who I choose to be."

"This couldn't be Windglass, more likely a wind-bag, pretending to be someone important to give some meaning to his otherwise miserable life. I mean, look at him sitting there. It's like someone put trousers on a pig."

Windglass chuckled. "Trousers on a pig. That's a new one."

"Now how about that drink, old man?"

Suddenly Windglass' posture changed as he turned to face the men, the sad drunk suddenly gaining an almost regal bearing. His eyes became cold and calculating.

"Tell me, did any of you serve in Her Majesty's army? Because then I would be more than happy to buy you a drink."

The men shook their heads.

"Then I'm not buying any of you a drop of water. You best be moving on."

A tall, thin man at a nearby table stood up like he was at attention. "Sir, my name is Darren Wood and I served under you in Hoodoo as a private. I'd like to buy *you* a drink."

Ignoring the toughs, Windglass turned to the man suspiciously. A lot of men are happy to lie for much less reward than a drink. "What outfit were you with?"

"The 222nd."

"So you were under old Major Bloom were you?"

The thin man looked confused. "No, sir. Major Flat. I don't know who Bloom is."

"Good man and good answer. Bloom doesn't exist. You'd be amazed at what some people will say or do to take advantage of my better nature. Let me buy you a drink."

"But general, I said I wanted to buy you a drink."

"Nonsense. When it comes to a man who served in the Army, especially one who served in my command, I must insist on buying the first drink."

"So then you'll be buying drinks for all of us instead of the old windbag," the leader of the toughs said.

"I'm sorry, but I don't have enough money for that."

"But you've got enough to waste on some old drunk pretending to be someone he's not?"

"As I said, I served under General Windglass. And this is him."

"Windglass would never be in a piss-hole like this. I don't care about your army nonsense. If you're not going to buy me and my friends a drink, then just hand your money over to us."

"That's not going to happen." The thin man stepped forward, but the leader of the toughs shoved him and he fell to the ground.

Before the leader of the toughs could react, Windglass was off of his barstool and had his hand around the man's throat. The tough noticed several things. Windglass didn't look so frail and helpless anymore. The fingers around his throat held him in an iron grip. The old man was strong and he started to realize just how strong when the former military man lifted him off the floor so that his toes were dangling.

"The lad served his country and you try to rob him? I'll not be having any of that nonsense in my presence." Windglass loosened his fingers and let the tough fall to his rump on the wood floor. "Begone and this will be the end of it."

The leader of the toughs rubbed his neck and nodded to his crew as a pair of them jumped Windglass from behind. The thin man tried to step in, but the leader of the toughs sucker punched him in the jaw, knocking him down. The old man flipped one of his attackers and smashed his foot on the man's rib cage. Windglass caught the second in the throat with his elbow. Another man jumped on the old man's back, but Hornblower came up behind him and laid him out with a sap he pulled from his pocket.

The leader of the toughs and his last remaining companion rushed the general from the front. The two men considered themselves good fighters and dirty ones at that, but they had spent their pugnacious lives battling against other men whose only training had been previous fights. Instead of backing away, Windglass step forward, bringing both hands up on the sides of his attackers' heads and smashing them together. With a clunk, they fell to the ground.

Windglass turned to the first two men who had attacked him, as they were still conscious. "You take your friends out of here and don't let me ever see you again. If I do, you won't be walking away from me then. Do you understand?" The two men nodded. "The proper response is Y*es, Sir*."

The two civilians found themselves standing at attention and yelling, "Yes, Sir!"

The two men grabbed the pair that Windglass smashed the heads of and dragged them toward the door.

"You boys forgot one."

One of them laid his man outside the door then ran back to drag the one Hornblower sapped.

Windglass walked over to the thin man and offered him a hand up and once he was upright, slapped him on the back. "I appreciate the help. Now before I buy you that drink, what's your name, lad?"

"Former Private David Wood, sir."

Shared fights and drinks in combination tend to forge bonds and loosen tongues and this was certainly the case with David Wood.

"When I couldn't find any work in Thames, I moved my wife and children out here to Elkshire. My wife's brother was able to get me a job at the mill. Right now, we're staying with them until I save up enough for us to get a place of our own. Am I to understand that you are actually living in the old soldier's home, General? I thought that was a place for those who had no home left to go to. Her Majesty awarded you lands and a dukedom for your role in ending the hundred-year war."

"First, David, I've already told you to address me as Colonel."

"But you are a general."

"I was a colonel for over a decade and a general for less than two years," Windglass said. "I was a better colonel. And yes, I did get an estate and a title, but I find sometimes it is best to keep things simple and stay with people who know me best, like the Sergeant here." Windglass patted Hornblower on his back.

"Thank you, Sir," he replied.

A gawker came in the door and hovered near the former military men. Hornblower and Windglass exchanged a glance.

"This never bodes well," Windglass said.

A young girl ran breathlessly in the door, saw Windglass, and sprinted towards his table.

"Colonel, help us!"

"What is it, Karen?"

"Elkshire is under attack by sky pirates," the young girl said.

A bald man with a gold earring rushed into the bar in pursuit of the child. He had no shirt but wore a vest and held a large cutlass in his hand.

Spying Karen behind Windglass, he gave a yell and raised his cutlass as if planning to disembowel the former general. Windglass stepped forward instead of away and caught the man's forearm, locking it into his side. Windglass brought his elbow up into the side of the man's head. The would-be kidnapper crumbled and Windglass plucked the sword from his grasp before he hit the ground.

"Little miss, are there more of the likes of him about?" Hornblower said.

The girl nodded. "A lot."

"Sergeant, go and fetch the lads. Private Wood, guard this child."

"But sir, I have no weapon," Wood said.

Windglass raised his eyebrows, flipped the sword, and handed it to Wood grip first. "Now you do. See to it that you keep her safe."

"What are you going to do?" Wood said.

The Colonel smiled and balled his hands up into fists. "Teach these curs a lesson."

Windglass ran out of the bar and towards the commotion, the floating gawker following in his wake. He came straight across a sky pirate with a bandanna tied around his head, his hand clasped around a young woman's wrist and his cutlass pressed against her pretty throat.

"Unhand Miss McGuire," Windglass ordered. The man's voice had authority and the pirate's first reaction was to let go of the woman's wrist, but then he grabbed it back and pointed the cutlass away from her and towards Windglass.

"Go away, old man. We don't want you. We wouldn't

even get a shilling on the slave block for someone as old and wrinkled as you."

"Miss McGuire, do you remember the time I scolded you for the way you behaved when one of my lads winked at you?" The young woman nodded. "Now would be a most appropriate time to repeat the gesture."

Trudy McGuire swiftly brought her knee up into the pirate's groin, causing him the double over. She pulled her arm away and ran.

Gasping for breath, the pirate stood up straight and glared at Windglass. "She's going to pay for that, right after I kill you, old man."

"That's very unsporting of you. I'm not even holding a weapon."

"A pity for you, geezer."

Windglass looked down where a bunch of carrots had scattered in the dirt next to a basket, undoubtedly dropped when the pirate grabbed Miss McGuire. Windglass bent and picked up the largest carrot in his left hand and pointed it at the young man to distract the pirate as he pulled something from behind his back with his right.

The pirate shook his head. "You're daft, geezer. Do you think you're going to kill me with a carrot?"

"No, that's just my snack." Windglass snapped his right hand out. A metal rod made clicking noises and telescoped until it was five feet long with a sharp point on the end. Windglass stabbed the collapsible spear into the chest of the pirate before the man could even move the sword. "I'm going to kill you with this souvenir from Hoodoo. I just needed to ensure you were overconfident, so you didn't come at me before I was ready."

As the pirate's vest grew a crimson blossom, the raider fell to his knees and met the reaper, still unsure exactly what had happened. Windglass grabbed hold of the blunt end of the spear, then kicked the man's chest and so he fell off the pointed end. The old man bent down to pick up the cutlass from the dead pirate's hand and resumed moving toward the commotion. As he turned the corner, he saw an airship floating above the town square.

Sky pirates were rushing after the women and children, using their blades to slaughter any unarmed man who tried to stop them. The poor people of Elkshire had been caught unprepared for the onslaught. The town had little by way of defenses. This high in the mountains, most strategists never thought they would need them, but that had changed with the advent of airships.

Windglass ran towards the pirates' airship, but he wasn't a young man anymore. Nor was he anything approaching sober. He had been drinking so much for so long that he'd learned to function from day to day with no one outside of his band of former soldiers truly being able to notice the difference. While he could fool his neighbors, he could not fool his legs. His exertions back in the bar hadn't helped matters either. The former commander of Her Majesty's military forces stumbled and fell after he tripped over a cobblestone. Fortunately for him, the whiskey in his system mixed with adrenaline numbed him from the pain the fall should have caused him. A woman was screaming and standing over a fallen pirate. Another pirate was warily approaching her as she swung at him with a broom. A third came at Windglass but got a cutlass buried in his neck for his trouble. Leaving the blade, Windglass moved toward the woman.

She blocked the sword and hit the pirate in the head. He responded by splitting her broom with his blade.

"Help me!" the woman screamed.

At least he thought it was just one woman. It sounded like she was alone, but to Windglass it appeared as if she was one of twins being abducted by a pair of identical pirates. Windglass deemed that unlikely and closed one eye, then used his spear to knock the pirate's cutlass out of his hand. It wasn't so much purposeful as him trying to get his balance. The pirate–he was mostly convinced there was only one as the second had vanished when he closed his eye–let go of the woman and turned to face him. Windglass attempted to bring up his spear before realizing he had dropped it when he had dispatched the approaching pirate. Not wanting to miss an attack, he opened both eyes and the missing twin returned. Trying not to pick the wrong opponent, Windglass lunged forward with both hands balled into fists and aimed at the noses of each of the men he saw. He missed both, his hands passing by on either side of the man's head.

The pirate laughed as if this was the funniest thing he'd ever seen, but that was his mistake. Drunk are not, Windglass had decades of reflexes that even alcohol abuse could not destroy completely. The old man closed his eyes to listen to the laughter, then grabbed hold of the man's shoulders and head-butted him in the face hard enough that he heard bones crunch. He opened an eye to see one man crumble to the ground.

Windglass took several deep, steadying breaths and his double vision was gone when his lids opened. Grabbing the unconscious pirate's blade, he moved to retrieve his spear, but when he bent over to pick it up, he had to put his other hand on the ground to prevent himself from falling flat on his face.

"The pirates have my children!" The woman begged. "Please save them, Colonel."

The gawker flew in for a close up and Windglass grabbed hold of the flying machine and pulled himself back up to standing. The old man steadied himself, put a comforting hand on the woman's shoulder, and nodded. "You have nothing to worry about. We shall rout these ruffians and get back everyone that they've taken."

Windglass charged toward the town square and the airship hovering above. He stumbled again but kept his feet. The sky pirates had a precision operation, forcing their captives into nets connected to ropes which were then pulled up toward the deck of their ship. The sky pirates then followed, climbing up on knotted ropes.

By the time Windglass reached the square, only one pirate remained on the ground and was forcing a teenage girl named Adelia into a net. She managed to kick out, burying her foot in the kidnapper's groin. He doubled over in pain.

Windglass launched his spear, but the alcohol in his system again cost him his footing and he missed the pirate. The bearded man grabbed hold of the girl's net to ride up to the skyship. Adelia clawed at the pirate's face and bit his fingers.

He lost his grip but grabbed onto a nearby rope.

As the girl fended off the pirate, Windglass leapt up and managed to get his fingers in the net that held her, but his weight did nothing to slow the girl's ascent. He lifted up the cutlass and drunkenly swung the blade in an attempt to slice open the net so Adelia could escape, but the movement instead caused him to lose his and tumble down to the ground. A woven basket broke his fall, but stole his breath.

Windglass lay gasping as he watched the airship fly out of sight.

"Colonel, are you all right?"

"No, Sergeant, I am not." Hornblower and retired Lieutenant Jeremy Urwin grasped their former superior officer underneath the arms and pulled him up. "I was too… inebriated to stop them."

"Sir, you may be the greatest man I've ever known, but you're still only one man. There were many sky pirates," said Jeremy Urwin, a by-the-business sort, from his shined shoes to his horn-rimmed glasses.

"If the Colonel couldn't stop them, there must have been at least fifty," Sergeant Hornblower said.

Windglass shook his head. "There were at least twenty-one on the ground. I know because at one point I counted forty-two and divided by half. There were at least as many more on board. This was a shameful display by a former officer of the Queen's. Even if I was unable to stop the ship, I still had my hands on a girl they were kidnapping." Windglass sighed. "I would've saved her had I been younger."

"Or if you were not stumbling drunk," said an orange-skinned man with long black hair who was so tall that none of the other men's heads reached to his shoulder. The collective former soldiers gasped at the Hoodoo's words.

Just then, Wood came running up. "I got them to safety, Colonel." Wood stopped short when he noticed the orange man and pointed his sword at the Hoodoo's stomach. "Hoodoo! Shall I kill it, Colonel?"

The orange man laughed. "Not on your best day, Albioner."

Windglass waved Wood away. "Put your weapon down.

Plato is a friend."

"You're friends with a Hoodoo? I thought you conquered them. How could you be friends with one of the savages?"

"Windglass is friends with you blighters, too. Look around at your so-called Empire. And we are called the savages. Our culture predates the Albion Empire, not that it is so hard to do." The hoodoo looked right at the gawker when he said it.

It confused Wood, who had never seen a gawker off of the battlefield before. "What is he talking about, Colonel?"

"Hoodoo believe that they were once the only ones on this planet until beings from another world called the *aloff* placed humans here for their entertainment." Windglass pointed his chin at the floating gawker.

"What utter poppycock, right, Colonel?" Wood said.

The Colonel shrugged.

"But that still doesn't explain where this Hoodoo came from."

"Plato is my friend and has chosen to help keep me out of trouble."

"Windglass saved my family and my village. I owe him a debt of honor."

"I thought you wiped out the Hoodoo?"

"That was another tribe, the one that ruled the rest of us and the ones that killed Windglass' family."

"Enough about the past. What matters now is the present and how we're going to get those people back from the sky pirates."

A trembling woman ran up and threw her arms around Wood. "They took the girls."

"The sky pirates have our children? Colonel, we have to get them back."

Wood placed his hand on the Colonel's shoulder and he almost fell over.

"You're drunk? Is that why you didn't stop them? How could you fail in your duty?"

Windglass stepped up and placed his nose so that was practically touching the front of the former private's nose. "For one thing, Wood, I was not on duty. I am retired and therefore no longer have a duty. In fact, I drink because of what occurred during my former duty. I will not be lectured by some former snot-nosed grunt about what I choose to do with my personal time. Are we clear?"

Wood cringed and backed away. "Yes, Sir, but how are we going to get my two kids and the rest of those people back from the sky pirates?"

Windglass sighed and regained his composure. "Now is the part where we figure out just how we're going to manage that. Sergeant Hornblower, how are we for supplies and weapons?"

"Colonel, you know we are retired and had to leave all property of the Queen's military behind when we left the army."

"That may be true, but I happen to know that every week you sent a box of supplies home to your mother and during that time we lost several old weapons, ammunition, and an entire battlewagon that seemed to disappear a piece of the time."

Hornblower smiled. "Now that you mention it, I do seem to recall sending a few things to me Mum that might come in handy."

"Get me a complete inventory of anything that might be useful because every minute we stand here lets the sky pirates and their victims get further away."

"Well, as it turns out I do have a complete battlewagon, a number of rifles and ammunition, enough mess supplies to open a small eatery, and an observation balloon."

"I don't see how the pots and pans and such will help us, but get the battlewagon, the weapons, and ammunition, and bring the observation balloon along. It may prove useful. Put a rush on it and gather the rest of the lads."

Sergeant Hornblower ran off.

"Excuse me, Colonel, but shouldn't we send for the local constables or the Steam Table Knights?" Wood asked.

"Local constables are geared to track down sheep stealers and break up bar fights. The pirates would eat them alive. And while the Steam Table would have the resources, by the time a telegraph message reaches them, it would be days before they arrive. I'm afraid we are the only hope that those people have." The Colonel turned and fell onto his face as the alcohol in his bloodstream finally beat out the fading adrenaline. Wood looked absolutely terrified at what was his children's only chance of rescue.

Plato on the other hand, laughed. "Even a drunken Windglass is enough to take on twice that many pirates, little man, so don't worry. If he says he's going to rescue them, they shall be rescued."

A few minutes later, an armored battlewagon pulled up. Plato gently woke the former general from his mud nap and Hornblower opened up the back.

Wood's jaw dropped at the number of guns and ammunition that he was facing.

"How can you have these? Private citizens aren't allowed to own guns," Wood said.

The Sergeant laughed. "But we're not exactly private citizens, are we?"

"We aren't?"

"Why, of course not. Did you even bother to read your discharge papers? We are former soldiers of Her Majesty's army and, as such, we may be called at any time to again perform our duty for Crown and country. The least we can do is make sure that we can arm ourselves in case that need arises. And soldiers are not only allowed to carry guns but are expected to, correct?"

"I suppose so, but where did you get so many? And a cannon?"

The Sergeant waved his hand as if it was a ridiculous question.

"It was easy and I was doing the army a favor. These are old rifles. Command periodically orders old weapons destroyed when the new versions arrive. Keeps the gun makers happy. Destroying these beauties seemed a waste of resources, so I took it upon myself to make sure that we soldiers would never be caught with our trousers down."

"I thought they melted down the metal to reuse it in the new weapons."

"That much is true, to a point. They do meltdown guns, but not to make more guns. They use them to make artillery shells and ammunition. Is that any way for fine weapons such as these to end up after helping us soldiers fight for Her Majesty? I say not. Besides, what is the first thing they teach us in training about our rifles?"

Wood didn't even have to consider before he answered. "Take care of your rifle and it will take care of you."

"Correct. I'm simply doing what the army taught me."

"Perhaps that argument works for old rifles and sidearms, but I've never heard of recalls on cannons and battlewagons."

"True enough, but when the majority of Her Majesty's forces were pulled out of Hoodoo, a percentage of the weapons were turned over to the savages to police themselves as part of the treaty."

"Again, with calling us savages. Have you ever seen how you blighters behave?" Plato said.

"Fine, in deference to our resident savage, I'll call them natives. But I fought and bled and watched my brothers die in fighting the Hoodoo and I'd die before I let them get Lucile or Bernice."

"Who are they? Your wives or girlfriends?" Wood said.

Plato snorted. "No, this one just likes to name his toys. Bernice is the battlewagon and Lucile is the cannon. Actual people don't like Hornblower much so he instead becomes friends with objects."

"Are you insulting me ladies? Because it sounds to me like you are. Are you spouting fighting words at me now, Mr. Savage?"

"No, Sergeant, I am not, if only to spare you the embarrassment of losing to me once again."

By this time, the rest of the retired soldiers had arrived, making them sixteen in all.

"Into the wagon, lads," Windglass ordered. "We must be off. The wagon is swifter than an airship on a straightaway, but there aren't any straightaways in these mountains. We have our work cut out for us to catch up to the sky pirates."

Bernice took off with Hornblower at the wheel of the armored monstrosity. Many of the men sat outside on the roof to avoid the sweltering heat inside caused by the boiler. Two of the former soldiers stood by to feed wood into the boiler as needed. They drove in silence for some time. It was obvious Wood was worried about his children, concerned enough to break the silence.

"When we catch pirates, they will outnumber us and have the high ground," Wood said.

"Nonsense. At the Battle of Wasting, the Hoodoo outnumbered us five to one and we were the ones who were victorious in the end."

"Colonel, the facts you present are true enough, but do leave out a few details, such as having the vast superiority in firepower and having airships and battlewagons to get troops to surround them. In our current situation, we have no such support," said Major Sanders, who appeared to be well into his seventies, but still fit for a man of his advanced years.

"True. This time, the enemy has flintlock pistols and rifles and blades. We have multiple cartridge rifles. They may have the high ground, but we have the experience in combat," Windglass said.

"And what is this nonsense, Sanders, about us not having air support? We have air support," Sergeant Hornblower said.

"One observation balloon hardly qualifies as air support," Major Sanders said.

"Arielle is strong enough to carry two men and a basket, I'll have you know," Hornblower said.

"But you don't have a basket, do you?" Major Sanders said.

"Not as such, but we'll see what presents itself along the way."

"While I appreciate the enthusiasm, Sergeant, while you're driving the wagon, keep your eyes on the road," Windglass said.

"There isn't hardly any road to keep my eyes on. In fact, we left the roads a ways back. I'd call what we are on now at best a deer path."

"We've been riding for some time. How do we know are going in the right direction?" Wood said.

"We don't," the Sergeant said. "We're doing the best guess scenario from the direction we saw them take off in the assumption that the pirates are going to want to get to the captives to a ship to make the trek across the channel to sell them in Guale."

"Not anymore," said Captain Paul Ashdown, the type of ruggedly handsome man that one wouldn't want one's wife to spend too much time around for fear that thoughts of unfaithfulness would make themselves known. Ashdown had his eyes glued to the viewer on the periscope which went up above the wagon up to forty feet, making the Sergeant's driving a bit more challenging as he had to not only find surfaces to drive on but make sure there was nothing above them to rip the scope down or at least give the captain enough warning to put the scope down "I have visual confirmation of the sky ship."

As the battlewagon crested to the top of the peak, they all saw the pirate airship.

"Colonel, Lucile can make a shot and take those bastards down," said Sergeant Hornblower.

"And also make casualties of the innocent civilians on board. Negative," Windglass said.

The Colonel stroked his white mustache. "Roads up here barely deserve the name. It seems unlikely that we will overtake them in a direct course. From the looks, they are fighting a strong headwind which is bringing them west and slowing their eastward progress. From what I've heard of the slaving trade, they should be headed to the coast, but they aren't. Isn't Trout Run to the west of here?"

"It is, Colonel," Ashdown said. "As a matter of fact, it's the left at the next fork in the path."

"Think they're headed to Trout Run?" Hornblower said.

"I do. It explains why they are wasting steam fighting the wind and risking staying low along the tree line. They are going to hit another town. They want to ride in low over the trees so the people don't see them until it's too late. We need to beat them to the town, hide the civilians, and set a trap for these gutless slavers," Windglass said.

"But Colonel, if you're wrong, that means they get away with my children," Wood said.

The old man laid a hand on the young father's shoulder. "It

is a calculated risk, but a risk we have to take. The simple truth is at this point we have little hope of overtaking that airship before they reach the coast and unload their human cargo on either a larger airship or one designed for the water and take these people across the channel. But if my guess is correct, we may be able to wipe them out and free all of their prisoners."

"But what if you're wrong?"

"Then I'll lose some of the little sleep I'm still able to get every night. Sergeant, get us to Trout Run and don't spare the steam."

The former soldiers arrived at Trout Run as most people were ending their workday.

As the battlewagon drove through the streets, crowds began to follow in their wake until the sergeant stopped in the center of the town square and most of the men got on top of the battlewagon.

"Citizens of Trout Run, lend me your ears," Windglass said

"Why should we listen to some old man in a stolen battlewagon instead of reporting you to the Army for such a blatant theft?" said one of the town men.

"Curb your tongue! Do you know who it is you are addressing?" Hornblower said.

The man laughed. "No, and why should I care?"

"This is…" The Sergeant realized what he was about to say and looked at his former and still commanding officer. Windglass nodded his permission. "General Duke Reginald Windglass. I'm sure Her Majesty would be amused by you reporting a theft of one of the gifts she granted him upon his retirement. "

"Gifts?" Wood said, but Major Sanders elbowed him in the ribs.

The eyes of the man who'd spoken opened wide, as did those of many around him. "Begging your pardon, Duke Windglass. I did not realize who you were."

"Not to worry about your brashness, but we're here because sky pirate slavers are on their way to Trout Run. We probably have less than half an hour before they arrive. I need you to gather up your old, your women, and your children and get them to safety. If you know of any caves outside of town or other places that pirates would not think to look, I advise you go to them now. If any of you men here served in Her Majesty's army, I am conscripting you for one more campaign. We are going to lay a trap for these pirates. I know many military men take souvenirs when they leave the service. I need you to go get those blades and guns and make them ready for battle once more."

Wood was surprised not only by the ease with which the former general commanded people who had never met him before but by the speed with which they rushed to follow his instructions.

Preparations had barely been completed when the pirate airship rose out of the nearby woods, seemingly appearing out of nowhere. Wood was able to appreciate the fear the pirates had worked hard to strike into the hearts of those they attacked. He hadn't seen the front of the airship until now. It was painted with a skull.

As the ship neared the outskirts of Trout Run, ropes were thrown over the side. Ten pirates lowered themselves down and walked in on the West Road, followed by a gawker. The pirate ship circled the town and dropped pirates at the points where the North, East, and South roads entered the town, again each with their own gawker trailing after them.

Windglass himself was able to appreciate the tactics. By coming in from each direction, they herded the people towards the center of the town, as they had in Elkshire. The airship then rose up toward the town square to wait for the herding of the townsfolk who were to become their living plunder.

The dropped pirates made their way towards the town square, their cutlasses at the ready.

On the West Road, ten pirates looked side to side and then back at each other.

"Where is everybody?" one of them asked.

"There!" another responded, pointing to a woman walking along the street in a bright pink dress.

The two pirates ran after her. One grabbed hold of her arm and spun her around. "You're coming with us, wench."

Both men creased their brows when the bearded face of former Sergeant Hornblower greeted them from beneath the bonnet.

"I'm afraid my whole day is booked stopping pirates," Hornblower said.

One of the pirates brought his cutlass back and lined up a swing that could have decapitated the former soldier, but instead, he lifted both hands out of his sleeves and fired at the two men with a pair of revolvers.

The pirates grabbed their wounds and dropped. Their eight companions turned and drew their flintlock pistols from their belts and pointed them at the Sergeant.

"I advise you to put your weapons on the ground and surrender if you want to live," Hornblower said.

"You can't fool us. You don't have any more shots," said one of the pirates.

"That is a foolish assumption. Not all guns are flintlocks, but even if I didn't have any more shots, these good people do."

The pirates looked around to see a group of men pointing flintlock pistols and rifles at them from windows, the roof, and one even who had been hiding in a barrel.

The pirates may have been vicious, but they weren't stupid. They placed their weapons on the ground and then lifted their hands above their heads. The soldier, the townsmen, and one woman who had taken her late husband's pistol, tied up the pirates.

The West Road may have been secure, but the East Road was not. Two men lay in ambush for the pirates—the Hoodoo Plato and the bookish Lieutenant Urwin.

These pirates were concerned by the lack of townspeople to conscript into slavery. There was a large crate placed in the middle of the street and the men gravitated toward it, trying to figure out what it was. While they all had their backs to the street, former Lieutenant Urwin stepped out from the doorway and pointed a rifle at the pirates.

"Throw down your weapons and surrender or be destroyed."

The pirates spun, saw only the one man with the rifle, and laughed.

"That's an army rifle? No matter. You don't have enough bullets in there to kill all of us."

"You are wrong. I take it that you refuse to surrender and have chosen instead the option of being destroyed?"

"You'd be correct at least about the not surrendering part," said a pirate whose hair was cut into a Mohawk.

The Lieutenant leaned back against the doorway and put his rifle butt down on the ground. "All right, if that is your choice." There was a crack as the wooden crate burst open and the Hoodoo Plato burst out, a pair of shining katana-style blades whirling in his wake as he spun among the ten men slashing and stabbing. Before the first man could even turn around, they were all dead, their lifeblood seeping out onto the cobblestone street.

Plato examined each of the men to make sure they were no longer in the land of the living.

"They're all dead," Urwin said, rolling his eyes.

"Too many good men have died assuming a still opponent was dead instead of lying in wait." The tall orange man was not convinced of one man's state and plunged his sword through the pirate's throat.

"It'd be easier and a lot safer for you if you didn't insist on me giving the enemy a choice," Urwin said.

"But it would not be as honorable. Even those who do evil, can turn their lives around and do good."

"You mean like you and your Hoodoo tribe?"

"I was referring to you, blighters."

The lieutenant chuckled as the Hoodoo cleaned his blades.

The pirates on the North Road kept together as they walked into Trout Run, which was quite fortunate for the defenders who were led by Major Sanders. As the invaders stepped on a portion of the road that was covered in dirt, four heavy men leapt off the roof. They held onto ropes which were hooked to pulleys, which in turn were hooked to a large fishing net. As the men got almost to the ground, other townsfolk grabbed hold of the ropes and pulled. The ten pirates were launched into the air and found themselves dangling in the net.

When facing down pistols and guns in their helpless position, the pirates made the wise decision and drop their blades and flintlocks through the net onto the street. The lot were secured easily.

The pirates on the South Road made it further than their companions and were looking through windows in search of the townsfolk. Unfortunately for one middle-aged man, he had not hidden himself well behind the window. A pirate took his cutlass and ran it through the window and into the man's throat.

"They knew we was coming!"

The townspeople on the South Road, along with Captain Ashdown, leapt out from their hiding spots street to engage the pirates in hand-to-hand combat. The townsfolk were tradesmen and fishermen. Even the former soldiers among them were many years removed from combat. The pirates, however, were used to fighting on a regular basis and each of them killed the first man that came at them. But the townspeople outnumbered the pirates and got smarter and started firing. When the gun smoke cleared all the pirates were down or dead, but so were eleven of the defenders.

All the gunshots in different parts of the town alerted the pirate captain, a man who went by the name Blondbeard, that something was amiss.

"Lift us up and get us out of here," Captain Blondbeard ordered.

"But Captain, our men aren't back aboard the *Skyhawk* yet," said the navigator, a short pudgy man.

"Look down them roads. Do you see any of them? A bit unusual, no? Someone should have signaled us by now. The men won't be coming back." He directed his speech to the gawker floating next to him.

"But without them, we have only a skeleton crew."

"Better to get away than be part of a crew of corpses. If I have to repeat myself, you'll be walking the plank from the highest altitude the *Skyhawk* can obtain."

"Yes, Captain." The navigator pulled the lever that normally brought them higher up into the sky.

"Why aren't we moving?" Blondbeard said.

"I've got the engines at three-quarters, yet we're holding still!" "They must have anchored us somehow."

Another of the pirate crew looked over the side. "They've got some sort of spears piercing the hull with ropes on the end. Cor! They've got a cannon pointed right at us!"

"Go down the side and cut us free," Blondbeard said.

"But Captain, I'll fall."

"I'm surrounded by thickos. Tie yourself off and we'll lower you down."

The pirate did as he was ordered as he got to the anchoring rope a shot rang out. The pirate went limp and his cutlass fell from his hand.

"Ahoy to the ship. Surrender or be destroyed," Windglass shouted.

"And who would be ordering the surrender of Blondbeard the Pirate?" The captain had posed, putting his hands on his hips. Instead of addressing his comment to the ground he looked straight at the gawker floating in front of him.

"The former General Reginald Windglass."

The gawker moved in for a close-up as the pirate's face turned white.

"The Army was lying in wait for the *Skyhawk*? But how would you even know we were coming?"

"Shall we discuss the terms of your surrender?" Windglass said.

"Never! You obviously are here to free the slaves we have in our hold. If you do not let us go, we will start throwing bodies over the side of the ship."

All the crew had moved to the starboard side when Windglass announced who he was because even pirates wanted to get a glimpse of a legend. That left the port side unwatched as the survey balloon Hornblower called Arielle rose up on the port side with the former Private Wood tied on, holding a repeating rifle Hornblower had modified to hold seven shots, one more than typical. Wood quickly fired at the row of pirates. Six shots rang out. Six pirates fell. Blondbeard pulled a flintlock pistol from the bracer wrapped tightly around his chest.

"That's six shots. Now you're just a sitting duck. Any last words?"

"You should not have touched my children." Wood then fired the seventh and final shot, catching the pirate between the eyes.

Wood then pointed the rifle at the remaining pirates. "I reloaded," he bluffed. "Now if you don't want to end up with a bullet in your head like your captain, land the ship and surrender to General Windglass and you'll get to live."

The navigator nodded and moved the lever down, landing the *Skyhawk* in the town square. The surviving pirates were all bound and placed in a makeshift jail before any of them realized the Army wasn't actually there.

Windglass and his loyal friends boarded the *Skyhawk*. Wood opened the door on the floor, then lowered the ladder down, but Windglass was the first one into the hold.

"My good people, you have been rescued. My name is Reginald Windglass and we will be getting all of you home to your families."

The girl who Windglass failed to save leapt up onto the old soldier, wrapping her arms around his neck and kissing his face repeatedly.

"I knew you would save us!"

"Yes, Adelia, you are welcome, but this is most unseemly child."

"Child? I'm a woman. I've already had three proposals."

"Why haven't you accepted any?"

"None of them were worthy of me and I'm not about to settle. Did you kill the pirate who took me? If not, I want another shot at the cur."

Windglass smiled. "Good lass. We'll go have us a look."

The second man down the ladder was Wood and his children threw themselves into his arms as well. The former soldier wept at the reunion. Windglass casually wiped away a tear at the sight of a man reunited with his children. The rest of his men all had the decency to be looking elsewhere when their Colonel turned back around.

When all the prisoners were out of the hold, many of the townsfolk offered to take them in, offering them food and a place to stay the night.

Windglass and his irregulars walked the deck of the *Skyhawk*, along with Adelia who trailed behind and refused to leave the former Colonel. Windglass ran his hand along the side rail.

"She's a good ship. It's not her fault Blondbeard and his ilk used her for evil."

"No, sir, it's not," Major Sanders said. "What will we be doing now? Use the ship to ferry the people home?"

"More than likely, but I was thinking."

The men all stood at attention in silence, some of them smiling. Even Adelia stood like a soldier. When the Colonel started thinking it might be dangerous, but it was never dull.

"We could interrogate some of the pirates that we have prisoner," he said. "In all likelihood, they were headed to the coast to meet with their pirate allies to unload their cargo to be taken across the Albion Channel and sold. That means that there are others in need of rescuing." No less than three gawkers hovered around the men. "I propose we take the *Skyhawk* as spoils of war and go after these villains, to free their prisoners before they can be sold into bondage. It will surely be dangerous."

"Not the least of which is that none of us know how to fly this thing," said Plato.

Windglass laughed. "True."

"What is also true is that we are no longer with the Queen's Army. Technically, only the government can own an airship. We would be criminals, even if we were just stealing from other pirates," Lieutenant Urwin said.

"What you say is correct, Lieutenant, but we've all sworn an oath to serve and protect this country and its citizens. Criminals we might technically be, but what kind of cowards and oath breakers would we become if we did not at least try to save these innocents from such a terrible fate?"

The men and woman stood in silence.

"This is not a sanctioned operation. I will not order any of you to join me. However, if you do join, the rules of old will apply, especially military discipline. Now, who's with me?"

"I am!" All the men answered in unison.

"Me too," Adelia said.

"But you are a girl," Hornblower said.

"She has told me she is a woman and gets quite temperamental when she is told otherwise," Windglass said.

"But there are no women soldiers," Hornblower said.

"But the soldiers are commanded by Queen Theodora who is a woman," argued Adelia. "And there is now a Steam Table Knight–Lady Thistle–who is a woman. Please give me the chance to prove myself, Colonel."

Windglass stroked his chin.

"You can't be seriously considering her request?" Major Sanders said.

Urwin pushed his glasses up on his nose. "Army regulations…"

"We're not in the army anymore," Windglass said. "Thus we have the option of using common sense instead when the need arises."

"Among the Hoodoo, women have the same opportunities as men and each is treated equally by their abilities. Women are even soldiers," Plato said.

"Bunch of savages," Hornblower said.

"Adelia, I will give you a chance. One. You will be a private in rank. Not only will you have to obey orders to the letter, but you will have to pull your own weight. Do you think you can do that, lass?"

Adelia saluted. "Yes, Colonel."

The girl held her hand at her head until the Colonel returned it.

Plato looked around at the *Skyhawk*. "The woman is a good addition, but there is more to running this ship than we few can manage alone. Perhaps you can enlist the aid of some of the townsfolk to join you in your quest."

"Good idea."

"Begging the colonel's pardon, but after we rescue those people, will we come back to return the former prisoners to their homes? Including my children? And will you continue to use the airship? Because I would be proud to be part of your crew. Mill work is all right, but a bit dull. Which leads me to my next question, will your crew be paid?"

"Of course, we shall ensure that everyone, especially your little ones, gets home. As for pay, pirates tend to have treasure, which would be considered spoils of war. I see no reason why every member of the crew shouldn't get a share."

"I did notice a locked treasure room below decks," Hornblower said.

"And I noticed the lock appeared to be broken after you looked at it," Plato said.

"Enough. Hornblower, return whatever it was you will undoubtedly tell me you didn't take. Plato, bring us the navigator so he can train us how to fly the ship. The rest of you gather up the townspeople so I can speak to them about joining us. We shove off in an hour."

There has long been a debate among certain obscure and drunken literary scholars about whether **PATRICK THOMAS** was raised by Cthulhu, a leprechaun in a Manhattan bar, or two human parents. What there is no arguing about is that Patrick is the award-winning author of 40 books including the beloved fantasy humor *Murphy's Lore series* (9 books from *Tales from Bulfinche's Pub* to *The Mug Life*), as well as 2 books in the future space adventures in the *Startenders* series.

The Murphy's Lore After Hours spin-offs star the half pixie/ogre Terrorbelle (*Fairy With A Gun, Fairy Rides The Lightning,* and *Terrorbelle The Unconquered*); the former demon-possessed serial killer Agent Karver of the Department of Mystic Affairs (*Dead To Rites, Rites of Passage*); the cursed magi Hex (*By Darkness Cursed* and *By Invocation Only*); Vince Argus, the Soul For Hire (*Greatest Hits*); and Negral, a forgotten Sumerian god who works as Hell's Detective (*Lore & Dysorder, Bullets & Brimstone,* and the graphic novel *The Moon Maniac* with Blair Webb).

His *Mystic Investigators* paranormal mystery series includes *Shadows & Brimstone* (omnibus of *Bullets & Brimstone* and *From The Shadows* with John L. French), *Once Upon In Crime* (omnibus of *Once More Upon A Time* and *Partners In Crime* with Diane Raetz) *Mystic Investigators,* and *Mean Streets. Assassins' Ball* is his first traditional mystery, co-written with John L. French. He co-edited *Camelot 13, New Blood, Hear Them Roar* and was an editor for the magazines *Fantastic Stories of the Imagination* and *Pirate Writings.*

His other works include the steampunk *As The Gears Turn,* the space epic *Exile & Entrance,* and the *Bikini Jones* series. Patrick's darkly humorous advice column *Dear Cthulhu* has been running since 2005 and has 6 collections including *Cthulhu Knows Best* and *What Would Cthulhu Do?* The Dear Cthulhu advice empire has expanded from magazines and books to radio as Dear Cthulhu now broadcasts monthly on the show Destinies: The Voice of Science Fiction which is hosted by Dr. Howard Margolin.

Over 100 of his stories have been published in magazines and anthologies. His noir novella appears in *Murder in Montague Falls.* A number of his books were part of the props department of the *CSI* television show and *Nightcaps* was even thrown at a suspect's head. His urban fantasy *Fairy With A Gun* had been optioned for film and TV by Laurence Fishburne's Cinema Gypsy Productions. Top Men Productions has turned his *Soul For Hire* Story, *Act of Contrition,* into a short film.

He also writes books for kids as PATRICK T. FIBBS including the YA *Emotional Support Nifghtmare,* the midde readers *Undead Kid Diaries: Over My Dead Body,* the *Babe B. Bear Mysteries: Bad Hair Day, Joy Reaper Checks Out,* the picture book *Fushcia The Mermaid Who Loved Pink,* and the *Ughabooz* picture books *5 Silly Monsters Jumping On The Zed* and *On Top Of A Yeti,* and the early reader *Soggy Goes to the Beach.*

Please drop by www.patthomas.net or follow him at I_PatrickThomas at Twitter or www.facebook.com/PatrickThomasAuthor to learn more.

Help is only a Rainbow Away…

"Mix Gaiman's American Gods and Robinson's Callahan's Crosstime Saloon on Prachett's Discworld and you get an idea of Thomas' Murphy's Lore." -David Sherman, author of STARFIST and Demontech

"ENTERTAINING, INVENTIVE AND DELIGHTFULLY CREEPY." -JONATHAN MABERRY, New York Times and Bram Stoker Award Winning Author

"SLICK… ENTERTAINING." -Paul Di Filippo, ASIMOV'S

"HUMOR, OUTRAGEOUS ADVENTURES, & SOME CLEVER PLOT TWISTS." -Don D'Ammassa, SCIENCE FICTION CHRONICLE

PATRICK THOMAS

Being *CURSED* to wear a bikini
Won't stop this Hero
From *SAVING* the world

THE ADVICE
COLUMN TO
***END* ALL**
ADVICE COLUMN

One Last Chance to Save
Happily Ever After

Can a group of heroes including Goldenhair, Red Riding Hood and Rapunzel help General Snow White and her dwarven resistance fighters defeat the tyrannical Queen Cinderella? And will they succeed before a war with Wonderland destroys everything?

Their only hope to stop Cinderella's quest for power lies with a young girl named Patience Muffet who carries the fabled shards of Cinderella's glass slippers.

Roy Mauritsen's fantasy adventure fairy tale epic begins with *Shards Of The Glass Slipper: Queen Cinder.*

> "Fantastic...
> A Magnificent Epic!"
> -*Sarah Beth Durst* author of
> *Into The Wild & Drink, Slay, Love*

> "The Brothers Grimm
> meets
> Lord Of The Rings!"
> -*Patrick Thomas*, author
> of the *Murphy's Lore* series

> "Shards is a dark, lush, full-throttle fantasy epic that presents a bold re-imagining of classic characters."
> -David Wade, creator of 319 Dark Street

> "Roy Mauritsen's enchanting epic comes at a time when fairy tales are back in the forefront of our collective imagination."
> -Darin Kennedy, short fiction author

PADWOLF
PUBLISHING

In paperback & e-book
Find out more at:
shardsoftheglassslipper.com
padwolf.com"